All Days Are Night

PETER STAMM

Translated from the German
by Michael Hofmann

GRANTA

Granta Publications, 12 Addison Avenue, London W11 4QR

First published in Great Britain by Granta Books 2014 (ebook) and 2015 (print)
This paperback edition published by Granta Books 2016
First published in the United States by Other Press, New York, 2014

Copyright © Peter Stamm 2013
Translation copyright © Michael Hofmann 2014

First published in German as *Nacht ist der Tag* by S. Fischer Verlag GmbH,
Frankfurt am Main 2013

Peter Stamm and Michael Hofmann have asserted their moral rights
under the Copyright, Designs and Patents Act, 1988, to be
identified as the author and translator of this work respectively.

This book has been selected to receive financial assistance from English PEN's
"PEN Translates!" programme, supported by Arts Council England. English PEN
exists to promote literature and our understanding of it, to uphold writers'
freedoms around the world, to campaign against the persecution and
imprisonment of writers for stating their views, and to promote the
friendly co-operation of writers and the free exchange of ideas.
www.englishpen.org

This is a work of fiction. Names, characters, places, and
incidents either are the product of the author's imagination
or are used fictitiously, and any resemblance to actual persons,
living or dead, events, or locales is entirely coincidental.

A CIP catalogue record for this book
is available from the British Library.

1 3 5 7 9 10 8 6 4 2

ISBN 978 1 78378 009 9
eISBN 978 1 78378 008 2

Text design by Julie Fry
This book was set in Swift and Trade Gothic by Alpha Design and
Composition of Pittsfield, NH.

Offset by M Rules

Printed and bound by CPI Group (UK) Ltd, Croydon, CR0 4YY

www.grantabooks.com

ALL DAYS ARE NIGHT

All days are nights to see till I see thee,
And nights bright days when dreams do show thee me.

WILLIAM SHAKESPEARE

Half wake up then drift away, alternately surfacing and lapsing back into weightlessness. Gillian is lying in water with a blue luminescence. Within it her body looks yellowish, but wherever it breaks the surface, it disappears into darkness. The only light comes from the warm water lapping her belly and breasts. It feels oily, beading on her skin. She seems to be in an enclosed room, there's no noise, but she still has a sense of not being alone. Love is somewhere, filling her.

Time skips ahead. When she hears a whooshing sound, she opens her eyes. Now she is all alone. On the wall are rows of points of light that weren't there before. She closes her eyes; the whooshing sound fades and disappears entirely.

Later, a white-clad figure is moving by her side, hands soothingly extended, and disappears. Gillian feels a faint nausea that is almost pleasant, a wooziness tugging her down, back into sleep. Then it's light, everything is dazzlingly white. On the bedside table is a tray with breakfast. A smell of coffee, also of flowers. Very slowly her body awakens, she can feel her legs and her arm, pushing away the covers, the cool air on her bare skin. She feels little pain, only a sense of collecting herself and dissolving again, a slow pulsing. Next to her is a hand. It presses a button, it is her hand. Something lifts her up, she can hear a quiet humming. Breathing feels unusually easy, as though the air streamed into her body and left it again perfectly unhindered. A finger presses a green button, which has a little icon of a bell on it. Time passes.

The white-clad figure enters the room, approaches the bed, and, without asking, pushes the bedpan under her. And once again, the feeling of dissolving, the warmth streaming from her body.

Are you done?

Gillian says something; it sounds like a short bark. She feels she is only inhabiting a tiny part of her body, which seems very big to her, an empty building full of noises and uncontrolled movements. Each time she walks into a room, someone seems to have just left it. From somewhere she can hear conversations, laughter. Gillian dashes down a flight of steps, but once again she's too late. Napkins lie crumpled on the white tablecloth, with wine stains and breadcrumbs.

It's raining. Gillian wonders how long she has been lying here, but she expects no answer. She barely has strength for the question. She is sitting forward in bed, though she can't remember how she got into such a position. Suddenly she can feel something cold, first it's just a point, then it becomes a spine. It's dabbed on stroke by stroke, until she can feel it all, from top to bottom. There's a smell of alcohol. The radio is on, Gillian hears the time signal, a voice is speaking very quickly, she can pick out single words that don't make much sense. The UN special representative, the Mars probe *Beagle 2*, a semifinal victory in the Australian Open, an area of low pressure over the Bay of Biscay. Isolated showers. In her thoughts she repeats: the UN representative, the Mars probe, the area of low pressure, and she tries to grasp the connection between them. The cold sensation passes, and she no longer feels her back, the nightshirt drops like a curtain. Breathlessly, Gillian waits for it to rise again. Someone gives her a push, and she's running onto the stage, looking utterly disorientated. She turns to face the audience, looks into the footlights, and bows low. Three, four curtain calls, and the applause dies away, the brief moment of happiness is over. Gillian knows she was no good and that the director will tell her so, again. You were just acting, he will say. You need to live the part.

You can lean back now. Would you like me to leave the radio on?

Gillian tries to concentrate. Everything depends on her reply. She wants to be herself, to get up, but she can't. She can't move her legs, it's as though she has no legs. The radio stops, the nurse walks over to the window and draws the curtains. Gillian remembers: the rain, the low-pressure area. There must be a connection.

You should try and get some rest.

Rest from what? Something has happened. Gillian is hovering around it, the memory, she is moving closer and then getting farther away from it again. When she puts out her hand, the pictures disappear, and the blue water comes instead, the blue water and the empty space. But the other thing is there all the time, waiting for her. She knows there is a way out, and she will take it. Later.

The doctor pulled a chair up to the bed and settled himself on the armrest. In his hand he was holding a mirror, a toy mirror in a pink plastic frame. He asked her how she was doing.

Better, said Gillian. I'm getting there.

For the first time, she could remember.

Two days, he said, when she asked him how long she had been here. A month, a year—it wouldn't have surprised her.

We had to give you strong painkillers.

It wasn't a bad trip, said Gillian, and tried to laugh.

When she raised her hand, the doctor caught it with a sudden, gentle movement. Don't, he said. You shouldn't touch the place.

He launched into a description of her face, a dispassionate and technical listing, but Gillian couldn't quite understand what he was saying. Then he described the operations—the procedures—that would be necessary.

In six months there will be little or no trace.

Trace of what? asked Gillian.

It's relatively straightforward to put an ear back, said the doctor, but a nose has a great many delicate blood vessels. We are going to have to build you a new one.

It doesn't look very pretty at the moment, he said, but I still think it's a good idea for you to take a look at it.

Gillian closed her eyes, opened them, and put out her hand. The doctor handed her the mirror. She turned it this way and that, like a weapon she didn't know how to use. She saw the window, the many bunches of flowers in the room, the door, and the doctor's face. He smiled and asked her a question, but she missed it, she was still adjusting the mirror in space, as though looking for the right frame, and then she lowered her arm.

Is it very bad?

He nodded and said again, in six months' time. Someone who doesn't know you will hardly notice a thing.

What about someone who knows me?

We try to get as close a likeness as possible, God knows there are enough photographs of you. You'll be surprised, he added. Plastic surgery has made great strides.

How come I can smell coffee without a nose?

The olfactory centers are in here, said the doctor, bracketing his nose with his finger and thumb. He stood up. Would you like me to leave the mirror with you?

No, she said, and then, yes.

After the doctor was gone, Gillian picked up the mirror with a quick movement and held it very close to her face — as though to hide behind it.

She couldn't remember when they told her. Maybe they hadn't told her at all, and she just knew. Or guessed. Matthias was dead. There was silence, just the soughing of the wind in the trees, a dripping of water, and an erratic creaking sound, as of bent metal slowly relaxing. An orange light flashed on and off. Gillian felt no pain, only the sense that her face was wet. In her mouth she had the metallic taste of blood. She wasn't able to turn her head, but out of the corner of her eye she had noticed Matthias slumped over the steering wheel as though exhausted. He didn't move, he surfaced, disappeared, surfaced, disappeared. Even when there was light, his face looked dark, ruddy like the face of a drinker. If only she had been able to turn off the blinking light, then everything would have been all right, and she could have gone to sleep. But she couldn't move. And then, slowly, the pain came, in her chest, in her legs, in her face. It was as though she had never felt her face before, her features seemed to be bunched together like a fist. Matthias was dead. What was she going to do with all his things? What would she say to his family and friends? She thought of the food in the refrigerator, spoiling, and the potted plants drying out. Then she suddenly felt certain that Matthias was not dead. It's not possible, and the thought came as such a relief to her that she almost laughed out loud. It's not possible.

When Gillian came around, her father was standing by her bedside, in quiet conversation with the doctor. Gillian didn't listen. She closed her eyes and saw the hole in her face through which she had seen inside her head. She tried to raise her hands to hide, to protect herself. The covers were pressing down on her, she could hardly move her fingers. Suddenly breathing was a struggle too. She opened her eyes. The two men were still there. They weren't talking now, and were looking down at her, into her. It was more than Gillian could do to stop their looking or deflect or respond to it. She closed her eyes and ran away as far as she could. A silly game, a dance, a children's skipping

8

rhyme with endless verses. Then she heard her name, the doctor had said it. When she looked up at him, her eyes met her father's. Her father turned away.

How are you feeling?

She didn't say anything. She mustn't give herself away. She was hiding, and if she didn't move, they would never find her. She was capable of staying hidden for hours on end, in a wardrobe or behind the sofa, in the attic, before she realized that no one was looking for her. Then she would slowly start to creep back, show herself more and more blatantly, but it was as though her long period in hiding had rendered her invisible. Her parents seemed to see right through her. What a relief when she'd been standing for a quarter hour in the kitchen doorway, and her mother finally told her to set the table, as though nothing had happened. She heard the door and saw her father leave the room. The doctor followed him out.

Something was broken. Gillian remembered the feeling of despair when she held the pieces in her hand as though they could knit together and be whole again. She couldn't remember how the crash had come about. Only the feeling of weightlessness. Suddenly she understood that time had a direction, that it was irreversible. Her first memory was that sense of not being able to do anything anymore, of having no force and no mass. It was as though consciousness had already deserted her body, which accelerated through space, collided with something, was thrown back, hit something else in a ridiculous to-and-fro.

Gillian had always known she was in danger, that she would sometime have to pay for everything. Now she had paid. When the doctor asked her what she could remember, she had slowly moved her head from side to side. She wasn't shaking her head, she was looking for her memories on the white walls. But the things she saw there had nothing to do with her. Her job, her parents, Matthias—they were all from another life.

Everything is still there, she said, only I am gone.

The careful movements of the nurses, their deliberate smiles.

Tell me if this hurts.

Pain was small events that took place just in front of her face, a fireworks of stabbings that Gillian couldn't connect with herself. It was her body that reacted to it, flinching or convulsing. The nurse apologized, her voice sounded impatient. Gillian didn't want to apologize for her body, which was nothing but an heirloom. She was someone else, she had only just moved in here. When people came along, she opened the door to admit them. She watched her visitors, tried to read in their expressions what they thought of the address. If they seemed impressed, she was happy. It is nice here, isn't it. Bit of a work in progress, of course. She laughed. The nurse explained what she was doing, but Gillian wasn't listening. She tried to bring the pain into harmony with her face, to make one single image, but she couldn't do it. The picture was incomplete, the proportions didn't work.

Almost done now, said the nurse. There, that wasn't too bad, was it?

She left the room. The mirror lay on the bedside table. Gillian was thinking about the mirror, not her face. The mirror was the face she could hold up in front of herself. She put out her hand, hesitated, waited a moment longer, then took it. She played with it, turned it around and looked at its shiny back, a dim reflection of her face, a sense of intactness. If someone had looked at her now, it would be his face in place of hers. Then she turned the mirror around again and looked at herself for a long time. Earlier, she had sometimes stood in front of the mirror at home and gazed deep into her eyes. But her eyes were glass, the pupils black holes, and at the bottom of their impenetrable darkness was her body.

She tried with all her might to recognize herself in that flesh. She saw eyes, eyebrows, mouth, but they formed no whole. When the doctor or a nurse entered the room, she quickly put the mirror down on the table and imagined her image was trapped in it, so that she could hide from the looks of the others. She tried to make out disgust or horror in the expression of the nurse. But all she saw was a friendly indifference.

She looked at the faces of the nurses, tried to make herself a nest in them. In her mind she copied their expressions, pursed her lips, blinked her eyes, furrowed her brow. She involved them in conversation just to be able to watch their faces, and to be able to rest in them.

Her father moved a chair up to the bed. When Gillian turned her head, she could see him sitting there staring at an exhibition poster on the wall, three red dots placed diagonally on a green background.

Do you like that picture?

11

Three dots. She had picked her head up off the pillow. He looked at her quickly and then looked away.

John Armleder, she said. The artist's name suddenly sounded rather threatening.

They would pull off some skin, she didn't quite understand it, but the doctor wanted to take some skin from her forehead, and without cutting the blood supply, fold it down, and use it on the new nose.

Matthias is dead, said her father.

Yes, said Gillian, of course.

She had known it, she had seen him. The tears were running down her temples before she realized she was crying. Her father took a Kleenex from a box on her bedside table and wiped them away, in an unusually gentle gesture.

I'm sorry.

I could have been dead. Gillian had said the sentence over and over to herself, but it didn't have any meaning. The tears stopped as suddenly as they had begun. Her father dropped the Kleenex in the bin by the door and returned to the bed, settled down on the chair. He waited for a moment, then said he had a couple of practical things he needed to do.

Your mother was in your apartment and tidied up a bit.

Ever since she'd been in the hospital, Gillian had thought a lot about her childhood and the time after she'd left her parents' house, of drama school, the years on small provincial stages. She had a vague memory of how the story continued, her getting married to Matthias, her job in TV. She had come up with an ending, too, a scene in a garden, a sunny afternoon in summer, she was older now, but still attractive, there was a man, they were drinking white wine together and talking about old times.

Matthias is dead, said Gillian.

He had a blood alcohol level of 1.4, said her father. It sounded like a statistic, as though he had given Matthias's height or weight.

I'm tired, she said.

At least you're alive, said her father.

That's what people say. I'm not really sure…

He gave her a short look and then turned away.

Your friend said you and Matthias had had a fight.

Maybe, said Gillian, maybe we did.

Matthias had found the roll of film and taken it to the photo shop to be developed. Just before they were due to drive to Dagmar's to see in the New Year, he had slammed the prints down in front of her.

Who took these?

Gillian had taken the pictures without looking at them and slipped them back in the envelope.

That's nothing to do with you.

Matthias gave a humorless laugh. Of course you think it's perfectly acceptable to appear in photographs like these.

You can rest assured, she said, they're not going to be published.

Oh, so you took them for fun?

Maybe they were going to be a present for you, she said.

For a moment Matthias didn't say anything. What if

the guy in the photo lab kept a set of prints? he asked. But then you don't seem to care who sees you like that.

It was you who took the film to be developed, said Gillian, I never asked you to.

Matthias walked out. An hour later he was standing in the doorway in his dark suit and asking if she was ready. It was at that moment that Gillian lost all respect for him.

Okay, she said, we'll go. I'll just get changed quickly.

She went to the bedroom and put on her shortest dress, black fishnet stockings, heels. She put on scarlet lipstick and applied a little scent behind her ears, a sultry perfume Matthias had given her that she hardly ever wore. Matthias stood impatiently in the corridor.

When she passed him on the way to the front door, he hissed after her, where do you think you're going, a party with friends or a brothel?

Neither of them said a word in the car, and at the party he did his best to stay away from her. Gillian saw him in the distance with his gelled hair and shiny suit.

By two a.m. there was just a hard core of partiers left sitting around the big table, which was full of dirty plates and empty glasses. Matthias was the only man, he stood off, glass in hand, staring through the patio door into the dark garden. Dagmar, who had recently broken up with her boyfriend, was saying she was finding it increasingly difficult to see men as erotic objects. Even though the agreement had been that Gillian would drive them home, she had had a fair bit to drink. She agreed with Dagmar and said women simply had nicer bodies than men. Dagmar got up to go to the bathroom. She stopped behind Gillian, placed her hands on her shoulders, and kissed her on the cheek. Matthias opened the patio door and stalked out into the garden.

Matthias was arts editor of a magazine that was not noted for its coverage of the arts. When they first met, Gillian was still working for the local TV station. She had been impressed by the way he seemed to know everyone in the cultural scene. Their paths kept crossing, Matthias introduced her to people and talked her into going to openings and premieres. One very cold winter day they met at the premiere for a musical in a small theater in the city. After the show they sat together with some of the cast. Gillian talked to the composer for most of the evening. He had asked her what her name was, and she explained her mother was English. She had a sense the composer knew something about her that she herself was unaware of. When they all left the theater a little after midnight, the streets were full of snow, and an icy wind was blowing. Matthias said he had something he wanted to tell her. While the others walked to the funicular, he took her across the street to a small belvedere. The lights of the city glittered in the cold; even the stars seemed unusually close. Matthias showed her a memorial stone under a big linden tree and told her this was where Büchner was buried. He put his arm around her shoulder and told her the story of the poor child in *Woyzeck*, which Gillian dimly remembered from school. And the moon was a piece of rotten wood, the stars were little golden midges and the earth an upside down harbor. And then they kissed.

That was as far as things progressed that evening. They had parted at a tram stop and gone home their separate ways. It wasn't until the spring that they first spent a night together. Gillian had a couple of difficult relationships behind her and was glad that Matthias was straightforward and seemed to like her. He was very tender, but over time they slept together less and less often. They were both so busy that Gillian kept putting off the conversation she meant to have with him about it.

When he dropped to his knees and asked for her hand in marriage, she laughed and tousled his hair. It was in an expensive restaurant where they knew her and greeted her by name. First, the situation felt embarrassing, then she enjoyed it. Over the course of the following years, there had been a good many carefully orchestrated candlelight dinners and champagne breakfasts, and a surprise party for her thirty-fifth birthday with the guests in masks, weekend outings to spa hotels, overnight trips to specially decorated rooms for romantic couples.

Then she got the job as host, and suddenly she was making as much as Matthias. What really seemed to get to him, though, was the fact that when they were both reporting on the same events, she was the one who seemed to matter. Only now did Gillian understand that he might know everyone by name, but no one really took him seriously. When she did interviews, she sometimes out of the corner of her eye saw him standing around nearby. No sooner was the camera switched off than he would turn up and jump into the conversation. He would demonstratively throw his arm around her, or kiss her.

Is he really offended? asked Dagmar when she came back.

We had a fight this afternoon, said Gillian. She got up and went out into the garden. Matthias was on the terrace, smoking. What's the matter? Her voice sounded harsher than she had intended. Come back in, it's freezing out here.

He claimed she had been flirting with Dagmar. Was it her who took the pictures? he asked.

That's enough, said Gillian.

We're going, said Matthias, as though he hadn't heard her.

I'm not good to drive, said Gillian, and she traced a one-fingered spiral in the air. We can always stay with Dagmar.

You'd like that, wouldn't you, he said.

She left him and went back into the house. Someone spoke to her, but she didn't reply, and poured herself a glass of grappa, knocked it back, and then another. Are you planning on staying the night here? asked Dagmar. Perhaps we'd better, she said with a laugh.

Yes, said Gillian, we had a fight. But that doesn't matter now.

Her father stood up. Take some of the flowers, why don't you, she said. I've no idea who sent them all. Do you want me to read the cards? he asked. She shook her head. I feel like I'm a corpse in a mortuary.

That afternoon her mother called to thank her for the flowers. She asked when she could visit Gillian.

Ideally never.

Every intact face reminded Gillian of the destruction of her own. And she had the feeling she had to bear the horror of the other person, and comfort them with her own bravery. The only thing she could endure was the presence of the doctors and nurses.

Her mother didn't push it. She said she had been to

the apartment and cleared out the fridge and done the laundry.

Thank you, said Gillian, there's no need. My operation's tomorrow, and then we'll see. She said she was tired.

Take care.

You too.

She tried to sleep, so as not to think of the crash, the operation, Matthias.

In the afternoon her father came by again. He was very matter-of-fact. After the first operation she could theoretically go home, he said.

But it's probably advisable to stay in the hospital until you're half—

You mean until I look like a human being again? asked Gillian.

Until you can walk properly. When can you put weight on your leg?

They've inserted a plate, said Gillian. I should be able to walk in a week.

Anyway, it's very nice here, said her father. As good as a hotel. We can't offer you that quality of care at home.

I don't need looking after, said Gillian.

If anything crops up, give me a call. He got up and held out his hand.

I've got all I need, said Gillian. Say hi to Mom for me.

Try and understand her, said her father, almost in the doorway.

The anteroom to the theater was full of people in green scrubs. Gillian tried to pull herself upright to get a better view of them, but she didn't manage. She saw the faces from below, surgical masks and oblique eyes under brows that looked more salient from that angle, ridiculous little gauze bonnets. A face bent down over her, friendly eyes with smile lines, and a voice asked her how she was feeling. Always that question: how am I feeling. She tried asking herself others: What's left of me? And is what's left more than a wound? Can it ever heal? Will that be "me"?

Before she could reply, the face had moved away, and the eyes were looking elsewhere. The surgical masks wagged, and she heard sentences she made no effort to understand, instructions spoken calmly and quietly. She could sense the concentration and a kind of happy expectancy. It reminded her strangely of field trips at school. The class met at the station, one person after another joining the group, curt greetings, not a lot of talk. The surgeon said something, very softly. Movements still seemed to be unconcerted, everyone was busy and trying not to get in each other's way. The anesthetist told Gillian what he was going to do. The green shapes disappeared one after another, and for a brief moment Gillian thought she had been forgotten. That same instant she had a sensation of her legs being lifted, as if she were being shoved into a dark tube and left. She slipped down into the dark, faster and faster, lights whizzed past, sounds were suddenly very near, a bright bell sounded, an echoey voice slowed down beyond intelligibility spoke. Then it got very bright. She felt a hand gently touch her shoulder. The friendly face once more. Gillian's stomach knotted. She felt hands raising her, a shaking, heard metallic sounds. Lamps slid past her. Breathing became difficult. Her nose was blocked. She had a nose.

In the night after the operation, Gillian had nightmares. She couldn't remember what she had dreamed, but she could feel the nocturnal landscapes through which unseen people were moving, not talking but in some secretive way in communication with one another. If she opened a door, at that same moment the room behind it would come into being, when she turned away, it disintegrated.

The mirror wasn't where she had left it. The doctor was holding it in his hand when he walked into the room. He explained to her exactly what he had done, taken some cartilage from her rib area and shaped it into a nose, and then folded over a piece of skin from her forehead and covered it.

It's not very pretty just at the moment, he said. And maybe you can't imagine how it's all going to heal, but I can assure you...

She said it couldn't be any worse than what it was before.

I'm very pleased with you, he said.

Why? What have I done?

You've been brave.

Gillian had the feeling he was playing for time. She held out her hand. The doctor nodded and put the mirror down on her covers.

In three weeks, the skin should have taken sufficiently for us to sever its connection to the forehead, and then it will look better right away. And in another three months you'll come back to us. Now you've only got another couple of days here. After the second operation you should be able to work again. Do you have anyone to look after you?

No, said Gillian, and then on an impulse: Yes, it's no problem.

The doctor shrugged. Don't worry. It'll all turn out well.

Breathing was still difficult for Gillian. When she touched her top lip with her tongue she could taste blood and feel the rough gauze. The doctor went away. Carefully she felt for the mirror on the cover.

Before lunch she called her father in his office. Presumably he wasn't alone, there was a customer with him or a mechanic. He spoke quietly, and she sensed that he was in a hurry to bring the conversation to an end.

I was going to visit you, he said, I'll come and see you for a little bit after work.

I wouldn't, she said.

Really? he asked vaguely. Have you got everything you need?

I don't need anything, said Gillian, just to be left alone. You don't need to come.

I've got a lot going on, he said, in advance of the holidays everyone needs things done.

It looks even worse, said Gillian, and suddenly she was crying.

Her father seemed not to notice, he just said that was part of the healing process, the doctor had shown him pictures of the various phases.

It's not like with your cars, you know, said Gillian, where you can hammer everything out.

As if you knew, said her father. How are you feeling?

She had to laugh. Oh, I'm fine.

I'll come by tonight, he said and hung up.

The prospect of his visit made Gillian uneasy. It was conceivable that one day there would be a person with a different face, who would be her. But there was as little connecting her to that person as to the other one she had been before the accident. In drama school she had imitated faces and tried out gestures, and that had produced a sort of vague echo of whatever feeling was to be expressed. She turned down the corners of her mouth and felt a weak, unspecific sadness, she pulled them up and straightaway her mood brightened. Now, without a face, she couldn't do that. All sorts of feelings, relief, fury, grief, were just possibilities that couldn't be realized. Even other people's faces, those of the nurses and people in magazines, became illegible scribbles to her.

In the evening, Gillian's father hung his coat on a hook and hovered near the door. Then he approached her bed. He looked at her, not saying a word, gripped the bed frame, and reluctantly slid down onto the chair beside the bed. He didn't look at her while they spoke, he took her hand in his. His voice was quieter and more hesitant than during his other visits, and he only stayed for fifteen minutes.

After he had gone, Gillian called her mother-in-law. The phone rang a long time. At last a breathless Margrit picked up. When she heard who was calling, she fell silent.

I'm sorry, said Gillian.

It's not your fault, said Margrit.

Then she talked about Matthias's funeral, which had been beautiful, and she wanted to get Gillian's approval of the music and the restaurant where they had held the wake, and the text of the death announcement, which she read to her. She listed the people who had attended.

That's fine, said Gillian, I'm sure you did everything right.

It's too bad you couldn't be there, said Margrit.

Yes, said Gillian, I'll visit the grave as soon as I'm out of the hospital.

She got along with Margrit better than she did with her own mother. They talked a while longer, then Gillian said she was tired.

Call anytime, said Margrit.

Gillian wondered what Margrit and her parents would say if they saw the photographs. She was briefly alarmed that her mother might have found them in the apartment, but then she remembered that she had put the envelope away in her desk. She hadn't looked at the pictures herself. They were evidence of an evening she would prefer to forget. She still remembered her sense of shame, and then panic. She had pulled her clothes on as in a trance. Hubert stood in the open doorway. For the first time that evening, he was looking straight at her. She grabbed the film, which was still on the table. Then she walked off without either of them saying a word. She went to the train station. There was a man on the platform who stared at her as though she had nothing on, and she realized that she didn't feel up to taking a train or a streetcar home. She followed the

road into the city center, first through the industrial pre-
cinct, then suburbs she had never set foot in before. She
kept running into children in costume moving from house
to house. They were strikingly quiet. A few were accompanied by their parents, who hung back a little while the
children rang doorbells and asked for treats. It was fully
an hour before Gillian locked the door of her apartment
behind her. She was pleased that Matthias wasn't home
yet. She could have exposed the film and destroyed it, but
she had the illogical feeling that that would release the
pictures into the world. Instead she stashed it in her desk.
Then she ran a hot bath.

Matthias came home while Gillian was still in the
bath. She heard the door shut, and then he walked into
the bathroom and sat down on the side of the tub. He
played with a few remaining scraps of foam that were
drifting on the water. Gillian hoped he would leave, but
he started telling her about some editorial meeting or
other. She didn't listen. She leaned out of the bath and
reached for her robe. Matthias picked it up and held
it open for her. She stood and turned her back to him.
When she had climbed out of the bath, he put his arm
around her and kissed her. She twisted out of his embrace
and took a towel to dry her hair.

Over time, Gillian had almost forgotten about the
film, the only time she was reminded of it was when
she was looking for something in the drawer. She hadn't
asked Matthias what he was doing there. Maybe he was
snooping, but he could have been hunting for a perfectly
innocent paper clip or postage stamp. She wondered if
the lab assistant who developed the film might indeed

have run off some prints for himself. But in fact she didn't care either way. The woman in the photographs no longer existed.

The next morning, soon after breakfast, a policewoman came to the hospital. She was pretty and rather delicate looking. She shook Gillian's hand and introduced herself, Manuela Bauer from the cantonal police. She unpacked a laptop and a small printer. Gillian said she had no memory of anything, but the policewoman was busy with the machinery and didn't react. At last she was ready, sat in the chair by the bed, and began to type. She read Gillian her rights and said she didn't have to make a statement that would incriminate her or her husband.

It was an accident, said Gillian.

The policewoman said it was a case of grave physical injury.

Are you going to lock him up? asked Gillian.

The policewoman said of course there wouldn't be any proceedings against the deceased, but the case needed to be looked into just the same. She asked Gillian about the night of the accident, she wanted to know where they had been, and who else had been there. Gillian wondered if she would be made responsible for the whole thing if she confessed. She was the only person who knew the truth, and she wasn't obliged to make a statement. In spite of that she related everything as she remembered it.

And what was this fight about? asked the policewoman.

That's neither here nor there, said Gillian, it was silly. Anyway, I had quite a lot to drink in a short time afterward.

Did you ask your husband to drive?

It was obvious that I wasn't capable anymore.

You could have called a taxi.

Yes, said Gillian, we could have spent the night there too. But we didn't.

She had thought she didn't remember anything of the night, but as she spoke, quite a lot swam into her consciousness: she had to hold on to the car as she climbed in, Dagmar had tried to persuade her to stay. Matthias had said he would take back roads, that way they wouldn't get caught up in any police checks. Gillian felt sick, she rolled down the window, and the cold night air cut into her face. Matthias drove in silence. At that moment, she couldn't imagine they would ever be reconciled. Only the thought that that meant a separation oppressed her.

She must have dropped off. When she awoke, they were driving along a narrow forest road. The asphalt glistened with moisture, scraps of mist appeared among the trees. There were no other cars around. The radio was playing loud rock music. Gillian switched to a jazz channel and closed her eyes. Without a word, Matthias switched back to the heavy metal station. Was that the moment he lost control of the car? Her next memory was the weightlessness. And then the ghostly silence.

He struck a deer, said the policewoman.

It wasn't his fault, said Gillian, and she started to cry.

He shouldn't have been driving, said the policewoman, never mind what you said or did.

It was my fault, said Gillian, still crying.

I'm sorry, said the policewoman, sounding impatient, I can't help you. Legally, you're not to blame.

Before she left, she gave Gillian a leaflet from a victims' support group and asked if she wanted any support or psychological assistance.

Gillian shook her head. My parents are there for me. I need a new nose.

She tried to laugh, the whiffling sound she made disgusted her.

The taxi driver helped Gillian into the wheelchair and rolled her to the foot of the stairs, and then he went back to fetch her suitcase from the trunk.

It's okay, she said, someone will come down.

She had to lay the suitcase across her lap because she couldn't steer the wheelchair with just one hand. She took the elevator to the top floor. Luckily the thresholds were flush throughout the building. The silent apartment was a shock.

Hello, called Gillian, even though she knew there was no one there. Hello?

They had bought the place three years ago. The rooms were large, there were light parquet floors and full-length windows. In the living room there was a glass door that gave on to a balcony. From there you could see right across the city and the lake. A person standing outside could see into the living room, but that had never bothered Gillian. On the contrary, she loved the transparency and laughed when friends said she was living in a shop window or an aquarium.

Most of the other apartments were occupied by older people, who hung curtains in the windows and rolled down blinds every evening. Gillian hardly knew her neighbors. They exchanged greetings when they ran into each other on the stairs or in the underground garage.

The living room had been tidied, there was a bunch of withered roses on the dining table. Gillian had bought them two weeks before, to give to Dagmar, but she had forgotten to take them. Presumably her mother had left them there out of respect. The water in the vase was cloudy and stank, some of the petals had fallen. Gillian collected them in her hand, they felt satin soft. She crushed them in her fist, then she dropped them.

She rolled into the kitchen, which was spotless. That was her mother's way of showing love or care. When Gillian watched her at work sometimes, she was reminded of the stewardess her mother had once been. Every movement was practiced, even her smile looked experienced. Sometime Gillian had stopped confiding in her and started treating her with the same friendly inattentiveness as her father did.

The fridge was largely empty, a couple of jars of different mustards, some dried tomatoes in olive oil, dill pickles, a few cans of beer, and the bottle of Prosecco they kept for unexpected visitors.

Gillian tried to shift off the wheelchair onto the toilet. Instead of getting the crutches in the living room, she pulled herself up on the sink. Her legs gave way, and she crumpled on the floor and banged into the footrests of the chair, which rolled away and struck the wall with a loud crash. Sitting up, she pulled and shuffled her way to the toilet. If it had been up to the doctor, she wouldn't even have been given the wheelchair, but she had asked, just for the first couple of days. Still lying on the floor, she pulled her trousers down. The chill of the tiles heightened her need to pee, and she tried to pull herself up. Then it was too late, she felt the warmth of the quickly spreading puddle. She tried to get her pants off, but it was too late. Gillian felt nauseous. She stripped off, and mopped the floor with her sodden pants. All she could manage were a couple of dry sobs that didn't sound much like crying.

Her life before the accident had been one long performance. Her job, the studio, the designer clothes, the trips to cities, the meals in good restaurants, the visits to her parents and to Matthias's mother. It must have been a lie if it was so easy to destroy with a moment's inattention, a false move. The accident was bound to happen sooner or later, whether in the form of a sudden catastrophe or a gradual unraveling, it was coming.

She knew she could use her legs, the doctor had even encouraged her to. She heaved herself back into the wheelchair and rolled into the living room. On the sofa lay a book she had started a couple of weeks ago, a Swedish thriller. She found her place but was unable to concentrate and soon put it aside. She flicked through a fashion magazine. In the building opposite a window was opened, her neighbor shook out a duvet. Gillian knew her, vaguely. She shrank back, half naked as she was, but the woman didn't seem to have seen her, remained standing in the window for a minute or two, and looked down at the street. Perhaps she was looking out for the mailman or her children who might be back from school soon.

Gillian rolled into the corridor to get her suitcase. Back in the living room, she locked the wheels of the chair and slipped to the floor. She lay on the thick woolen carpet. That way she couldn't be seen from outside. It was warm, but she felt chilly. She rummaged in her suitcase for clean underwear and a pair of trousers, but the only things she found were dirty. She pulled a blanket off the sofa and rolled herself up in it. She longed to be back in the hospital where nothing more was demanded of her than that she be able to endure her pain. And even that had been taken away from her with the drugs she at first took gratefully and then increasingly refused. She had the idea that pain was part of the healing process, and that she needed to submit to it as part of becoming whole.

She propped herself up on her elbows and looked around. Nothing had changed, but the room had become strange to her. She asked herself who had bought these books, hung up these pictures. A silkscreen print by Andy War-hol, Marilyn, the same face ten times over, lifeless as an advertising poster. The minimalist furniture, the soulless accessories, carefully chosen from expensive design shops, souvenirs though they were connected to no particular memories. She rolled onto her back and looked up at the Italian designer lamp that seemed to hang just above her, dropped her arms, and hit the wheelchair several times. Locked now, it didn't move.

She crawled over to the enormous flat-screen, switched it on, and started zapping through the channels. She stopped at a nature program. There was a wide beach at twilight across which thousands of primitive creatures were creeping, looking as though they were put together from a round shield and a long sting or tail. From time to time one of the creatures would be picked up by a wave and dumped onto its back, and you saw its wriggling little legs and the way it tried to turn onto its front with little jerks of its tail. This fascinating spectacle only occurs for a few days each year, said the narrator adoringly. Horseshoe crabs have lived in shallow coastal waters all over the planet for over five hundred million years, and in all that time they have hardly changed. That's why they are occasionally called living fossils. In early summer they gather on the shores of their native seas to lay their eggs.

Gillian looked through the DVDs that were piled up beside the little TV console, but none of the films grabbed her. Finally she put on a DVD of one of her shows that she had had burned and never watched. She didn't like seeing herself on screen, it was only when something had gone wrong during one of the recording sessions that she watched the show.

She fast-forwarded it. She could make out the show's opening credits, a short introduction to the week's subjects, torn faces silently moving their mouths, smiling, a painting, ballet dancers. Now you could see the studio, a white room, or rather a white wall, with Gillian in the background seeming to float in white. The camera zoomed up to her at breakneck speed. She switched over to Play, and when the camera was very near, she froze the frame. There was her old face, wide staring eyes, mouth open in welcome. Gillian pressed a button, leapt forward from frame to frame. Her mouth closed and opened, but the expression in the eyes didn't change.

She never felt nervous before the programs and was surprised now by the look of fear in her eyes. It was as though the face could already sense its destruction ahead. An unexpected noise, a reflection, a sudden memory changed the expression, for a split second the cameras created a person there had never been before and who would never exist again. Twenty-five frames a second, twenty-five people who didn't have much more in common than their physical details, hair and eye color, height and weight. It was only the linking of the pictures that created the fuzziness that constituted a human being.

She pressed Play and lay on her back. She heard her voice, promising young talent, first one-person show, return to figurativeness. Gillian turned her head to the screen and saw herself announcing a film clip. Turned through ninety degrees her face looked thinner and younger. It looked unfamiliar, perhaps that was why she saw each individual feature with greater clarity, the lips, the dimple in the chin, the nose and eyes. She thought of Tania, who had never managed to make her up without passing some remark about her appearance, her heavy eyebrows, her thin lips, or her complexion. Her problem zones, she liked to say.

The woman on the television stopped talking, and her face looked tense for a moment that to Gillian seemed unending. At last the film began. The camera swung through an exhibition room, you saw life-size naked women washing themselves, getting dressed or undressed or doing chores. Although the poses were everyday, they seemed somehow classic. Then there was a close-up of Hubert's face, and his name was flashed up on-screen,

Hubert Amrhein, and in brackets his age, thirty-nine, the
same as hers. He talked about his work, about how he found
his models on the street, professionals didn't interest him.
Ordinary women, he said. They get undressed, I photograph them. It all has to happen right away, on impulse,
there are no prior agreements, no second chances. The
hunt for models was a large part of the artistic process,
he said. Of a hundred women he spoke to, maybe one or
two agreed. Of ten whose photographs he took, he might
paint two or three, often months later, long after he had
forgotten their names. While he spoke, some of the pictures were faded in. The editor's questions were cut out,
all you heard was Hubert's voice, always beginning again,
riffing and spieling. He didn't really know how he came to
choose his models, sometimes he thought they chose him.
It wasn't primarily beauty that interested him but inten-
sity, power, and pleasure, also lostness, aggression, fear. It
was like when you fell in love with someone. Usually you
couldn't explain that either. His smile looked at once shy
and conceited. Perhaps that went into the pictures, desire
and the impossibility of fulfillment.

Jerk, thought Gillian. Now there was a street scene,
passersby in a pedestrian neighborhood, filmed from a
slight degree of elevation. The camera fixed on a woman
and followed her through the crowd, a good-looking young
employee or businesswoman in a boring suit. Gillian tried
to picture her naked, but she couldn't do it. Sometimes
he would imagine one of his models happening to see the
picture of herself, Hubert said. She was strolling through
the city, stopped in front of the window of a gallery, and
saw herself naked in her apartment, washing the dishes

or vacuuming. I think she would probably recognize her kitchen fixtures before herself, he said. The photos are the work of seconds. They capture the secret life of our bodies while we're busy with something.

The final shot of the report was one of Hubert's paintings that showed a heavyset fortyish woman washing her foot in a sink. She was standing on one leg, the other was up. With one hand she was holding her ankle, with the other she was washing her foot. The fingers and toes were interlaced in a complicated way. Although the pose looked demanding, the woman seemed introverted, almost meditative.

Then they were back in the studio. Gillian and Hubert were facing each other for the interview. She had a few questions from her editor that she had written on index cards. She asked him about working with models, whether he gave them instructions or not. The movements need to be their own, said Hubert, that's actually not all that easy to achieve. I tell a woman to wash herself, and suddenly she's got her foot up in the sink. It would never have occurred to me. It's like a gift. Gillian saw herself smile and heard herself asking whether it was difficult to work with women who had no modeling experience. She stopped the shot. Now she looked disgusted. She clicked on until Hubert was next in a shot. The expression on his face was hard to interpret, a mixture of irony and sadness, or perhaps just conceit. She hit Play, and Hubert—as though coming out of a deep pause for thought—said, on the contrary. Professional models are practiced at reducing themselves to their bodies and wearing nudity like a garment. It's striking how some women change through being naked, and my looking at them. How the inside comes to the surface. It's a very private moment. Gillian had the sense he was saying these sentences specifically to her and not thinking of the TV audience at all.

Oftentimes nothing happens at all, he said. Generally I know before developing them whether the photographs will be any good, whether there's something useful there. Then who's the artist, you or the model? Gillian heard herself asking. It's not about the artist, said Hubert, it's about the work of art. And that has nothing to do with the model or the artist.

Gillian ran the recording back to the beginning and watched the whole interview again, frame by frame. She wanted to work out what had transpired between them. Ninety seconds, more than two thousand individual shots. The secret lives of our bodies, she thought. Hubert was a chatterbox, which made it all the more striking to her that he had said what she was thinking, or perhaps had even given her the thought in the first place. She had often caught herself adopting other people's ideas and taking them for her own.

The dialog between their two faces was very different from the one she had just listened to. From the outset there seemed to be a tense intimacy between them, often a barely perceptible smile flickered over one of their faces, and once at least Gillian caught admiration in her eyes, a girlish beam. Hubert's initial boredom gradually gave way to an expression of tenderness, which struck Gillian. Her own face in countershot looked down, as though his look confused her. She turned to face a different camera, and her face took on a rather foolish look of surprise and delight—she was introducing the next segment. Gillian stopped the film and took the DVD out of the player. On TV, it was still the horseshoe crabs, which were now back in their native element, water. And so each year they lay their eggs, said the warm voice of the speaker, and probably will continue to do so long after human beings have vanished from the face of the earth.

Gillian spent almost the whole day lying on the floor in the living room. Gradually she calmed down. She thought she was gaining strength, but when she pulled herself up, she felt dizzy. She sat there for a while and waited for it to pass. Then she picked up her crutches, which were lying beside her, and got up. It was easier than she expected, and she hobbled into the kitchen and ate a can of tuna and a couple of rice cakes she had bought months ago and hated. She drank a glass of Prosecco, even though the doctor had told her to stay away from alcohol while she was taking medications.

She went to the bathroom and opened her side of the medicine cabinet, which was stuffed with over-the-counter remedies and personal hygiene products. The woman who lived here was evidently terrified of bad breath, she gulped vitamins, presumably because she had a poor diet, she suffered from chronic headaches and an acid stomach. She was afraid of getting old and of cracked fingernails. A working woman who had more money than time, who bought expensive olive oil soaps in little boutiques and didn't get around to using them, and new toothbrushes before she threw away her old ones. It occurred to her that at last she would have enough room for all her stuff. Somehow she couldn't feel properly sad about Matthias. Sometimes she cried and cried without stopping. At other times she completely forgot that he was gone. They were always spending a day or two apart, being alone wasn't an effort. Gillian hadn't even been to his funeral, how could she know he was really dead?

She took off her blouse and bra. Looking down herself, it was easy to imagine nothing had happened. The accident had left her with a couple of bruises on her torso and some stitches on one leg, but other than that there were no signs on her body. Then she raised her head and looked at her face. In the hospital all she had seen were the wounds. What she saw now, over an almost intact body, took all her strength away. Her stomach knotted, and she crumpled to the floor. She crawled to the bedroom on all fours and flopped into bed. She felt her naked body, belly, waist, hips.

In the middle of the night Gillian awoke and couldn't go back to sleep. She got up and hobbled over to her office. She turned on the computer and went through her e-mails. She had more than three hundred items in her in-box. She quickly scanned the subject lines. Get well. Recovery. Sympathies. Forthcoming meetings and, days later, summaries of what had been said at them. She deleted all the messages. The in-box of her other address, the alias under which she had corresponded with Hubert, was empty. She Googled her name. Apart from a few short news reports about the accident, she found mentions of her TV show, a couple of articles that had appeared about her, a Wikipedia entry that some fan of hers must have posted, which was surprisingly accurate. She wondered how much longer you lived on in the Internet after you were dead. In a blog she came across a longish analysis of her work as a host. The blogger seemed to have a deep loathing for her. Her first thought was that it had to have been written by a man, but as she read on she saw that it was certainly the work of a woman. It sounded as though the author had met her personally, perhaps she was an artist or an arts worker Gillian had interviewed. When someone laid into her in the press, she at least knew who it was. Now she had the feeling of listening at the door of a room where she was being talked about. You won't please everyone, Matthias said sometimes when she had been criticized, but that wasn't it. She had never learned to keep a distinction between her work and herself, whoever criticized what she did attacked her as a person. At the bottom of the blog, comments were solicited. There were a couple of brief entries, broadly in agreement with the blogger, semiliterate statements full of misspellings and obscenities. Gillian briefly wondered whether to write something herself but decided against. She turned off the computer and opened the top drawer of her desk. The envelope containing the photographs was still there where she had left it.

Gillian hadn't met Hubert until immediately before the interview in the studio. In their initial conversation, he had laid into television for ruining his pictures, and eyed her shamelessly. Under the lights he asked her if she fancied having a drink with him afterward, and she declined.

Don't worry, he said with a mocking smile, I'm not thinking of painting you. It sounded like an insult.

By the time the recording was in the can, Hubert was already gone, and even though he had irked Gillian, she still felt disappointed. As Tania was cleaning off her makeup, she showed Gillian a little sketch he'd done of her, nothing wonderful, but Gillian was still annoyed about it.

Matthias wasn't home, so she fixed herself a sandwich and went into her office. She clicked on Hubert's website. The only entry under "News" was something about a group exhibition two years ago. Under "Who am I?" she found a photo of Hubert no bigger than a postage stamp, and a short biography. He had done an apprenticeship as a sign painter and then gone back to school. There followed a series of obscure grants and scholarships and group shows he had taken part in. Gillian clicked on "Gallery." There were five pictures of unoccupied rooms: an office, a bedroom, a living room, a kitchen, and a bathroom. In all the pictures it was nighttime, and the rooms were dimly lit. Although not much could be seen, Gillian still had the sense that there was someone in all the rooms, hiding in a corner or else behind the onlooker. Under the pictures it said they were crayon on paper, and their dimensions were fifteen by twenty-one centimeters. They seemed to be older than the series of nudes. Under "Contact," she found an e-mail address.

What was she going to say to Hubert? Why didn't he want to paint her? She spent a long time staring out the window, then she selected as sender Miss Julie, an account she had acquired in order to send anonymous e-mails. Each time she used it, she felt she really was someone else, as though she was back to playing the part of the irresponsible and yet determined character in Strindberg's play. She remembered the graduation show at drama school, and even some of her lines. When I really feel like dancing, I want someone who knows how to lead. There had been a lot of applause. When it was over she felt she could do anything. Looking at photographs of the production later, she saw a scrawny-looking girl with a silly face and staring eyes.

Not thinking anymore, she wrote to Hubert that she admired his work and was sorry not to see any newer pictures of his posted on his home page. After a brief hesitation she wrote: And as I've just seen, you're good-looking as well. She signed herself Julie, and pressed Send.

When she went to bed, Matthias still wasn't home. She woke at five and saw him lying beside her. She thought of Hubert and imagined meeting him in his studio. She knocked, he opened the door and showed her in. Without taking off her raincoat, she walked through the room and looked around. The studio looked like something from an old Hollywood film, with high windows, a potbellied stove, and a big easel. Hubert watched her with the blunt curiosity that had struck her in the course of their interview, and pointed to an old leather sofa. She ignored him and stepped up to the window through which she could see the rooftops of the city, and away in the distance, the Eiffel Tower. There were dark rain clouds in the sky, but at the horizon the cloud cover was broken and the sun shone through and illuminated the pale gray roofs of the city with its dazzling light. Gillian heard Hubert walk up behind her. Finally she turned around and took off her raincoat. Underneath she had on a simple black dress. He smiled, took her coat, and tossed it over a chair back. Then he picked up a notebook and a charcoal crayon from a low table, and started drawing. Gillian shut her eyes. She heard the scratch of charcoal over the paper.

Matthias turned over. Gillian quietly got up and went out onto the balcony. Although it was cold, she didn't feel it. It was daybreak, the birds were rowing, it all sounded as though she was in a glass bowl. In the distance she heard the occasional sounds of sparse traffic and the shunting of locomotives.

Before long, Hubert and Gillian were writing to each other every day. Matthias wondered why she was checking her e-mail all the time. She shrugged. Under cover of her pseudonym, Gillian asked Hubert why he wanted his models to undress when he claimed their bodies didn't interest him. He answered in almost identical words to those he had used at the interview, so she didn't believe him. He wrote about the encounter as part of the process, of the right moment, of the impossibility of planning. He asked her for her picture. Gillian wrote back that she didn't have any photographs of herself.

Have we ever met?

Gillian didn't see his e-mail till the next morning. She had to go to Hamburg for a couple of days to record a feature about an elderly writer who had produced a kind of autobiography. Her flight didn't leave until midday, and she was still in bed when Matthias left for work. He kissed her goodbye.

She had slept badly and felt depressed without knowing why. Even before her first cup of coffee, she sat down at the computer. She told Hubert that she didn't want to model for him. She had imagined him taking her photograph in her apartment and it hadn't felt right. Not the nudity, but his presence in her apartment, his looking around and making a picture of her life. No hard feelings.

She drank her coffee and smoked a cigarette. While she showered, she imagined Hubert painting her portrait. She looked around his studio. He pointed to an old leather sofa. Without taking off her coat, she sat down. He took a chair, sat down facing her, and started sketching her. After a time he put down his sketchbook and appeared irresolute. At last he said, very softly so that she barely understood, she could change behind the partition.

When Gillian reappeared, naked, from behind the partition, Hubert was just loading film into a big camera. Not looking up, he asked her to lie on the sofa with a book. He peered into the camera's viewfinder, she couldn't see his eyes, but sensed his cold, prying look.

Gillian packed her traveling bag. She still had time, and checked her e-mails. Hubert had written back already. He wrote that if she didn't want to be photographed in her apartment, they could meet at his studio. You're giving yourself away, she thought, you're changing the rules as you're going along.

Their e-mails were batted back and forth in double-quick time.

Are you alone?

You wish.

So you are.

Now you're taking advantage of me.

How so?

You're imagining me.

What alternative do I have if you refuse to show yourself to me?

Why do you only paint women? And why naked?

This time it took longer for an answer to come. His answer disappointed Gillian. She thought a moment, typed a question, deleted it. Wrote it again.

Do you sleep with your models?

When she fired off the e-mail, there was another one from Hubert. He wrote that the model's nakedness created upset, disturbance, erotic tension. Art was the harnessing of this energy in a painting.

Gillian regretted her question now. Again, Hubert's answer took a while.

Shall we meet?

That's unprofessional.

Shall we meet?

You're repeating yourself.

Life is repetition.

No.

Then what do you want?

Gillian thought. She typed her answer, read it back, and smiled as she pressed Send. She didn't wait for his reply and switched off the computer. The sound of the ventilator ceased, and the apartment became very quiet.

In Hamburg it was raining. Gillian took a taxi from the airport to the author's apartment. The film team was already

there, and the author was getting annoyed because the
cameraman wanted to rearrange his living room. He also
refused makeup, even though he had probably worn it
hundreds of times. Gillian explained that it was to allow
him to look his most natural. He seemed at least to like
her, and over time he unwound, and even started flirting with her a bit. They filmed him sitting at his desk and
in front of his bookshelves, out walking along the water-
front, in a smart café he would never dream of going to, as
he explained. Gillian asked him to write something down
for her, but it turned out he had nothing to write on. She
lent him her black Moleskine, and he scribbled something
in there. Then they trooped back to his house to film the
interview. Gillian sat beside the camera. When she opened
the notebook to review her questions, she saw what he had
written: This engenders such a clichéd view of the writer:
television is the pits. She didn't flinch and asked her first
question.

The author seemed offended that he was getting more
critical attention, and more readers, for his autobiography
than for his ambitious experimental oeuvre.

Even though this book is just as fictitious, he said.

And what is reality?

If it's reality you want, I suggest you look out the
window.

Then why write?

He looked at her with a pitying smile. For professional
reasons, a colleague of mine used to say. And another said
it was lust, greed, and vanity that motivated him. In my
own case, it's presumably...

The soundman said he had picked up a noise in the

background, could he possibly repeat the last few sentences, but this the author refused to do.

That's the thing with reality, he said, you can't repeat it to order, you can't correct it. Perhaps we should read more books.

Would you do something else if you had your time again? Gillian asked.

The writer was suddenly angry and said he was tired, and gave monosyllabic replies to her remaining questions. At the end of four hours, Gillian said goodbye. She would manage to knock her material into a four-minute feature, but it would have even less to do with reality than the three hundred and fifty pages of the autobiography (not really) under discussion.

While in Hamburg, she didn't check Miss Julie's e-mail. She no longer felt comfortable with her part in the correspondence.

When she got home four days later, though, she did. Hubert had written to her twice, once immediately, moments after she had turned off her own computer, and then the next day. In the first he offered a detailed description of how he would kiss her. He had assembled a pretty accurate picture of her, and wrote about her cropped hair and slender waist. In the second e-mail he apologized for the first. He said he had allowed himself to be carried away and was sorry. Gillian didn't know which of the e-mails to be more upset about. She decided she would meet Hubert. She wrote that she didn't want him to paint her or kiss her, but she would agree to have a drink with him. As a venue she suggested a café in an outer suburb where she had once met a curator. She looked at the time.

I'll be there at seven tonight, she wrote. You'll have no trouble recognizing me. Yrs, Julie. Hubert's reply came quickly, and was friendly but reserved.

Normally Matthias didn't get home till late. Gillian scribbled a message on a Post-it, she had to go back to the office, she couldn't say when she'd be back. She spent a long time wondering what to wear, and in the end decided on the most unspectacular things she could think of, a pair of tan cords and a white T-shirt with lace trim. She knotted a gray sweater over her shoulders. She didn't put on any makeup, even though she didn't normally set foot outdoors without at least a dab of powder and some mascara.

Gillian was early. There was no one in the café except two women and a young couple who were preoccupied with themselves. The women looked at her curiously, perhaps they recognized her. She took a table at the back and ordered a mint tea.

Hubert turned up shortly after six. When he spotted Gillian, he seemed relieved. He walked up to her table and smiled.

Oh, it's you, I might have guessed.

Gillian hadn't got up, he held out his hand to her. He seemed less sure of himself than in the TV studio, at any rate Gillian liked him much better. Hubert didn't say anything, and Gillian didn't know what to say either. In the end he asked her why she called herself Miss Julie.

After the Strindberg play, said Gillian. It was a part I played once. In my drama school graduation show.

The waitress came over. Hubert smiled at her and ordered a beer. When she came back with it, he took it from her with a little pleasantry and had a sip right away. The waitress walked away, you could tell by her walk that she knew Hubert was looking at her.

Do you like her then?

He apologized. I can't help seeing a potential picture in every face.

I had the sense it was more her bottom you were looking at, said Gillian. What do you see in my face?

He looked at her attentively. I don't know, he said. I always watch your program.

Really?

Your face is too familiar to me.

Then look at it more closely, said Gillian. She liked it when Hubert was looking at her with his keen, appraising look.

Your complexion isn't as clear as it seemed to be in the studio, he said finally, that must be the makeup. Your nose is a bit shiny. And you have unusually heavy eyebrows for a woman.

Gillian winced. I could have done without the detail.

I like the little hairs on your neck, said Hubert, and the mobility of your features. The way you sometimes open your eyes very wide. Are you nearsighted?

A little bit.

Hubert asked her why she wanted to see him. Gillian shrugged.

They were silent again, but it wasn't the disagreeable silence of two people who have nothing to say to one another. Gillian's cell phone went off. She looked down at the display and declined the call.

Will you show me your pictures?

Sure, he said, and went over to the bar to pay.

Although it was only late September, autumn was already very much in the air. It was almost dark outside, and distinctly chilly.

I've got my car in the car park, said Gillian.

Hubert gave her directions. During the drive, he asked her what she did in her free time. A bit of exercise, swimming, jogging, said Gillian. And I read a lot. What about you? She hadn't had a conversation like this in a very long time, and it made her smile. In a minute you'll be asking me about my taste in music.

The drive took less than a quarter of an hour. Hubert's studio was in an old textile works on the edge of the city. To the south was a dark wooded chain of hills, the slopes in the north were not so high. The valley drew in here, and it was dotted with ugly industrial buildings. The main building in the textile works was a wreck, its roof stove in, the windows boarded up. The walls were propped by a heavy steel scaffold to keep them from collapsing.

They crossed the yard to a side building. The sky was still bright, and there was a thin sliver of new moon. As Hubert and Gillian approached the building, a security light came on. Hubert unlocked the graffitied metal door, switched on a light, and led Gillian down a narrow corridor past a number of doors. His studio was at the back, a big, almost empty room with a paint-spotted linoleum floor. The walls were in an uncertain yellowish color, in some places you could see gray marks where shelves had been once. On the ceiling there were halogen bulbs that bathed the room in a chill, garish light. On one side of the studio were tall windows, the blinds were down. Along one wall were metal shelving units full of bottles and tubes, brushes, stacks of books, and sketch pads. There was a sofa, a couple of old kitchen chairs, a mattress in a corner. On top of a small fridge was a single hot plate, with a beat-up aluminum saucepan on it. Side by side along one wall leaned three evidently recent pictures like those in the exhibition, one was still unfinished. Next to them were the backs of half a dozen canvases, protected by clear plastic sheeting. A large empty easel stood in the middle of the room. Hubert took a couple of folders from the shelf and laid them on a table improvised from two wooden blocks and a length of chipboard. He opened them one after the other and quickly flicked through sketches, begun and completed drawings, as if that wasn't the purpose of their being there. Rooms, bodies, body parts, sometimes he turned one of the drawings around and looked at it as if for the very first time. He said a few words, perhaps he was talking to himself. The last folder he pushed aside unopened. Gillian saw the name Astrid marked on it. Then Hubert went over to the canvases that were propped against the wall, pulled off the plastic, and turned them faceup onto the floor, one after the other. Gillian stood next to him.

Most of my newer stuff is in the exhibition, of course, he said, all I've got here are a couple of older pictures.

All were of the same woman in various positions.

Who is she? asked Gillian.

He didn't reply. They were both silent now. When she wanted a little more time, Gillian placed her hand on his to delay it. It felt like they were peering through the sky-light of a strange apartment.

Very nice, said Gillian, when Hubert propped the pile back against the wall. Her phone rang again. She switched it off without looking at the display. Hubert coughed nervously and took a step away from her.

Are you interested in seeing the photographs as well? he asked.

She nodded.

He said he couldn't offer her much in the way of refreshment. Beer, a glass of wine, tap water.

Beer is fine, she said, and sat down in an old armchair into which she disappeared. Hubert took a couple of cans of Czech lager out of the fridge and poured them carefully into two large glasses with gold rims. He looked concentrated, as though it were a very demanding task. He brought her one of the glasses, took a chair himself and moved it to about ten feet from Gillian. As he sat down, he took a sip of beer and then set the glass on the floor next to him.

She said again that she liked the paintings, but he seemed not to want to talk about them. He made minimal replies to her questions and took sips of beer in between. Finally he got up and fetched an old slide projector from the corner of the room and perched it on a wobbly old barstool. He switched off the overhead lights, moved his chair closer to Gillian's armchair, and pushed the first slide tray into the projector.

Without a word, Hubert went through the photographs, one tray after the other. There were hundreds of nudes, women ironing, dusting, reading, making coffee.

There were dozens of shots of each woman. To begin with there was an amused expression on many of the faces, later on they looked more serious and stopped staring into the camera.

Gillian got up, went over to the window, and sat down on the window seat. Hubert didn't notice. She saw his silhouette and the images of the naked women on the wall. She imagined his face, pale in the reflection of the slides, his cold, critical gaze. She felt reminded of a photograph of a cinema audience she had seen once, incomplete faces with staring eyes and mouths opened in laughter. That was always how she had pictured her viewers.

In the next tray were pictures of a small woman with wide hips and large, pendulous breasts. She had short blond hair and hairy armpits. Both her posture and her facial expression had something theatrical about them. She hung washing on a low rack in a tiny bathroom, baby things and men's socks. She took a book from a shelf, hunkered down on the floor, and swept up with a dustpan and brush, maybe crumbs from biscuits she had given her child. The apartment was cluttered and untidy. In the last pictures, the woman looked close to tears.

She looks terribly lonely, said Gillian. Do you have any idea what you put these women through?

They agree to take part, said Hubert, switching the trays. Even in their nakedness they try not to reveal themselves. They hide behind their movements, their smiles, their way of exhibiting themselves.

Gillian was surprised that she didn't seem to get used to nakedness, as in the sauna or the shower at the gym. The more pictures she saw, the stranger the bodies became to her. A big mole, a fold of skin, pubic hair shaved back to a narrow strip, everything acquired exaggerated significance. The bodies fell apart, looked disproportionate, ungainly, ill made.

Is it like that for you as well? she asked.

You're starting to see them, said Hubert. That's the way I paint them, detail by detail, surface after surface. Even when I'm taking the photographs, I try not to be overly present. That's why I use a camera with a big viewfinder. When the models look into the camera, they see only their own reflection in the lens.

He had clicked rapidly through some pictures of a young, gangling woman, then stopped at one where she was looking at herself in a mirror. The woman's arms were hanging down, and her stomach was slightly protuberant. Her gaze looked critical, as though dissatisfied with what she was seeing.

Could perhaps do something with that one, he said, although mirrors are tricky.

What good is it for the woman, if she never sees the picture? asked Gillian.

Nothing, said Hubert. She's just the model. I'm not a portraitist.

And why do they take part?

I've no idea, he said. Maybe they have a need to be recognized in some way. He switched off the projector. Are you tired?

Gillian nodded.

I'm going to stay here awhile longer. Shall I walk you back to your car?

Yes, please, said Gillian.

It took her a while to find the way home. It was ten, later than she'd supposed, but traffic was still heavy. She felt disappointed, and annoyed with herself for being disappointed. He could at least have asked her to sit for him. The thought had a strange attraction.

While she was waiting at a light, she switched her phone back on. She got three text message signals. At the next light, she read them. Two were from Matthias, the third was from Hubert. She deleted them all without answering.

Gillian woke early. She was in pain again, but she didn't want to take any more pills. She stepped out onto the balcony in her dressing gown to smoke a cigarette. It was raining, and a strong, cold wind was blowing. She could hear some birds, but not as many as usual. The thought of birds sheltering from the rain, cowering in shrubbery somewhere, feathers ruffled and heads tucked in, moved her in a sentimental way. It got sneakily brighter, but the sky remained gray and the rain kept falling.

The fear set in quite unexpectedly. It seemed to come from outside, but it had nothing to do with Matthias's death or the accident, more the rain, the gray skies, and the shapelessness of the beginning day. Fear is the possibility of freedom, a sentence she had read once long ago and without ever understanding it, never forgotten. She still didn't understand it, but it seemed to describe exactly what she felt. In front of the building was a sandbox, a dismal parody of a children's playground, under a gray cover. The clattering of the rain on the polyethylene was very close and loud as the voices of the solo birds against the city's backing track. It was odd that rain always seemed to take Gillian back to her childhood, as though it had only ever rained then. She was ten or twelve, it was early morning, and she was on her way to school. She could hear the sounds of the rain on her hood, the drips splashed her face.

Gillian, she spoke her name out loud. She thought of the girl who had just graduated from drama school and had got her first engagement at an obscure provincial theater. She had played a dwarf in a Christmas pantomime, a serving girl in a comedy, and Rebecca Gibbs in *Our Town*. She told George about the letter Jane Crofut got from the preacher when she was ill. The envelope was addressed to Jane Crofut; The Crofut Farm; Grover's Corners; Sutton County; New Hampshire; United States of America, Continent of North America; Western Hemisphere; the Earth; the Solar System; the Universe; the Mind of God. You don't say, said George, who never got anything. And still the mailman had delivered the letter. Each time she said that sentence, it brought tears to her eyes.

It was a time when everything seemed possible, but freedom unsettled and scared her. She didn't suffer from stage fright, oddly, she never had, but a sort of fear that was worse after the show was over. Her boyfriend had been taken on at another theater, but they had never bothered to break up. They telephoned less, and then stopped entirely. Gillian was left to her own devices, she lived over a pizzeria in a little apartment where it was always too warm. She had no friends outside the theater, and none in it really either.

It took her a while to discover that she wasn't a good actress and never would be. She played women who gave themselves, who loved unconditionally, who sacrificed themselves, but she couldn't take any of the roles quite seriously. A part of her always watched herself acting. I can't regret, or flee, or stay, or live—or die! The little miss marched resolutely out the door, but the audience surely realized she wasn't going to the barn to hang herself, but to the dressing room to take off her makeup.

Only after she had entered journalism did she start to feel more secure. She got the job in television and then she started playing the beautiful and successful cultural correspondent for the viewers, for the media, for Matthias, and for herself. She avoided making crass mistakes, Matthias played along, basically he was the better actor. They were continually in demand, giving information, playing themselves. Their voices were louder, they moved differently in public. When they got home, half soused and tired, and stood side by side brushing their teeth in the bathroom, Gillian sometimes had to laugh at the two faces in the mirror. Even the laughter was part of the performance.

Gillian felt slightly sick from her cigarette. She put it out and went inside. She stopped briefly in front of the coffeemaker, then she went into the bedroom and lay down again. The window was open a crack, and the rain was audible only as a steady hiss. She spent all day in bed, delaying trips to the kitchen or bathroom as long as possible. Her pains had let up, but that didn't make it any easier, they had battered her back into her body, had made her boundaries all the more distinct. Gone with the pain were her points of reference, and now Gillian had to go to the trouble of finding them all again. She leafed through old photo albums. There were family albums, with pictures of her as a little girl, photos of holidays and birthdays, family portraits that barely changed over the years. These albums held the first pictures of elementary school productions, Gillian as Mother Mary, as Snow White, as a cat in a musical. Eventually her story detached itself from the family's. Everything concerning her profession was in a separate album, which Gillian had started. Theater programs, interviews, photos taken at parties, reviews, all clipped and pasted. The first page, the one that in the other albums bore a name or dates, was empty.

She read an interview she had given shortly after she had taken on the television job. Every week the same questions were put to a different person. The journalist had been perfectly pleasant, they had met in a café. Each time Gillian was stumped, they had made up the answers between them. When did you first make love? One afternoon. What would you most like to know? What my friends really think of me. What was the saddest moment in your life? They were both stumped by that one. Then the journalist had suggested: My death. And that had to do.

The life in those magazine pictures was inexplicably more personal and more concrete than the interchangeable family snaps in the other albums. In the interviews Gillian was asked about things she never discussed with her parents. Alongside these compressed and edited conversations, those she had at home seemed alarmingly banal. Sometimes her mother would talk to her about things she had read her daughter saying. Is it true that you don't believe in God? Gillian didn't know. It's just an interview, she would say, you have to tell them something.

Once or twice she had complained about becoming a celebrity, but in fact she had loved being recognized on the street.

At the back of the album were some clippings she hadn't stuck down yet. A write-up of her wedding, a double-page spread with photographs of the service and the party afterward. Gillian was astounded that Matthias hadn't made a fuss. The journalist and photographer hardly stood out, they integrated themselves better into the wedding company than some of Matthias's friends or Gillian's relations. And they were restrained too, only asking for the occasional shot or a few words. When Gillian saw the piece in the magazine a week later, she had the feeling the whole celebration had been staged. After that she became more wary. But then, after she had been gone from the magazines for a while, she missed the attention, and she agreed when asked for a feature about her home life. Matthias and her in their tidied apartment, reading, cooking, eating, or standing dreamily out on the balcony. We've been mugged, she thought, this isn't our apartment, that isn't Matthias, this isn't me. When she saw Matthias's expression, it suddenly seemed to her as though he was a part of the conspiracy, and had known about it all along.

The following day the sun shone. It was cool outside but almost too warm in the flat. The doctor had told Gillian not to go out in the sun, but she didn't want to go out anyway. For lunch she cooked some pasta. Afterward, she ordered food from an online grocery. She filled her virtual basket with things she had steered clear of so far, frozen meals, sausages, potato chips, pastry, white bread, ketchup, and mayonnaise. She bought enough to last her three weeks and paid with her credit card. Gillian started to sort through Matthias's clothes and shoes. She stuffed them into big garbage bags. It was difficult, on crutches, to get everything into the spare room. She emptied the contents of Matthias's desk into a cardboard box. Margrit had told her to do whatever she thought best. Sometimes she sat there for minutes, staring at a piece of clothing or some other item.

The deliveryman from the online store came toward evening. There was a ring at the door, and Gillian buzzed him in. When he rang again at the top of the stairs, she called through the door to leave the things outside. The man stood there for a moment and then went away. Only when Gillian heard the engine of the delivery truck downstairs did she cautiously open the door.

She ate a lot over the next weeks. She watched TV, surfed the Net, slept late. Her parents called her on the landline, and when she didn't pick up, on her mobile. Gillian said she was fine, she needed quiet, and she promised to visit them, next week, or maybe the week after.

Will you call if you need something? asked her mother.

I need time, she said. It's not about you.

She stopped answering the phone, she didn't even look at the display when someone called. She deleted her e-mails as well, without bothering to read them. She waited for Hubert to get in touch, but he didn't. Presumably he didn't even know anything had happened to her.

At night, Gillian dreamed of men attacking her and raping her and violating her. Her body exploded, her flesh flew in scraps through the air, the walls were stained with her blood. It was dark in the rooms, and yet everything could be clearly seen. In the middle of the night she woke up. She listened to the darkness. It was perfectly still, but she heard the emptiness just the same. She thought about the times at the end of recording sessions when the soundman said, atmosphere, and everyone froze, so that he could record the silence for a minute.

The days went by like the weather in a constant back-and-forth. It got cold, then warmed up overnight. Once, a lot of snow fell in the space of a few hours, but it all melted away within a day or two. Gillian no longer felt bored. Some mornings she didn't even get the newspaper out of the mailbox. She spent a lot of time thinking about Matthias and their former life together, but she still couldn't deal with the fact of his death. Grief came quickly and unexpectedly, a sudden stab of pain that made her reel.

For days she had worn the same pajamas, she didn't wash or shower, and she lived entirely on junk food. She watched her body change as she put on weight and developed spots on her back and her chin. For the first time in years she was aware of her body odor.

One sunny day she thought she would go for a trip. The late-afternoon light was as golden as it was in autumn. She rode the elevator down to the basement and followed the passage into the underground garage. She kept stopping to listen, but she couldn't hear anyone. Her dark green Mini stood where it always stood. She drove to a wood on the edge of the city and parked near a recycling station. A man was coming out of the wood toward the parking lot with his dog. Gillian crouched down and waited. The man opened the door of his car, which stood a couple of spots away from hers, and the dog jumped in. When he had driven away, and there was no one else around, she climbed out and set off. The path led along the edge of the wood. In its interior there were still a few scraps of leftover snow. After a while, Gillian saw a couple approaching with Nordic walking sticks. They were perhaps two hundred yards away. She stopped and looked around. Behind her was a woman pushing a stroller. The underbrush beside the path was fairly dense and difficult to penetrate. She kept her arms up to shield her face, branches scratched her hands. Thereafter it got easier. The ground was thickly covered with dense leaf mulch that gave underfoot. Gillian heard voices, and then she saw through the underbrush that the couple and the woman with the stroller passed each other. She waited a moment longer and then plunged deeper into the wood. The light fell diagonally, making long shadows. Sometimes Gillian stopped and contemplated the silver bark of a tree that looked like the hide of an animal, or a piece of tree root that was worn smooth by the elements. She laid her hand on the cool wood, feeling tiny unevennesses. The terrain became flatter. It was already starting to get dark, from the nearby zoo she heard animal cries. When she got back to the parking lot it was dark and the street-lights were on.

The following morning Gillian awoke early. It was still dark. She had no sense of her body, only when she moved did a shape gradually come to her. She turned her head to the side, felt her cheek brush against the soft pillow-case, then a leg under the duvet, her other leg, numb, the sole of her foot, the chilly floor, a slight feeling of dizziness. She passed through the rooms as though the apartment were her body, a big prone body, too heavy to pick itself up.

After her first cup of coffee she slowly came around, and under the shower her body knitted itself together to what it was. She vaguely remembered the time she was still growing. Her hips widened, her breasts deepened. It was like one long inhale, a picking herself up. Now she exhaled, for a long time she had done nothing but exhale, sometimes she had the sense of not having any more air in her and still having to go on exhaling.

Every other day or so, Gillian had to go to her doc-tor to get her dressings changed. In the waiting room, the other patients avoided her eyes. When the doctor said the wounds were healing well, it sounded to her like mockery. After the dressing had been changed, she often went for a drive around the city. Behind the wheel she felt invisible, only waiting at a light sometimes she noticed the driver of a car in the next lane eyeing her and

quickly looking away when she turned. She was drawn
to empty spaces, drove to the industrial park on the edge
of the city, parked her car at the soccer stadium. There
was no one around, only a couple of building machines
parked on the gravel. Around the perimeter was a tall
wire fence, the gate stood open. She walked in, climbed a
wide flight of steps. The stadium was much bigger than it
seemed from outside. The stands were empty, tiers of colored seats, blue, orange, gray, and green. She stood there
for a while, looking down at the playing surface and
trying to imagine the scene when there was a game on
and the stands were full of spectators. Another time, she
drove up to the top floor of a multistory parking garage.
The morning had been dry, but it started raining again
at midday. The walls of the garage were cement, with
wide spaces through which a powerful wind blew. Gillian
got out and made her way among the handful of parked
cars. She spun on her own axis, made wide sidesteps as in
fencing classes at drama school, leaps forward and back.
She occupied the space, as their speech tutor had taught
them to do, put out the flat of her hand as though to push
the walls away. She accompanied this with long, drawn-
out hissing. She felt excited, she didn't even know why.
The space seemed to be too big, it afforded no resistance.
In little pattering steps she ran to one of the openings
and looked out at the industrial buildings, at the multi-
lane highways packed with traffic bordered by trimmed
poplars, at the mountain away in the distance, dimly visible through the downpour. She felt cold.

When she returned to her Mini, she saw a man sitting
in one of the parked cars. He sat there motionless. Their

eyes met, and Gillian wondered if he had been watching her entire performance.

The day before the second operation, a Sunday, Gillian visited her parents. She hadn't seen her mother since the accident. When her mother opened the door and saw her, she turned aside and started crying. Her father stepped up and with an expression of annoyance pushed her mother out of the way.

Come on in, he said.

Her mother said lunch was almost ready, and she disappeared back into the kitchen. Gillian followed her.

The sounds of silverware on the plates seemed so deafeningly loud that Gillian could hardly hear what her parents were saying. The two aged faces contorted themselves to ugly grimaces as they chewed their food, Gillian looked down at her plate, broke up her food in small pieces, which she swallowed, almost without chewing them.

Aren't you hungry at all?

What's that?

You're hardly eating anything.

I'm not hungry. Gillian put down her knife and fork and stood up. I'll be back in a minute.

As she was shutting the bathroom door behind her, she saw her father get up to refill his plate.

She sat on the toilet and waited. It was cold in the house, she was shivering. Her father kept the thermostat way down, her mother had whispered to her in the kitchen. Her father hadn't finished eating, but her mother had already started to clear the table. They had their coffee in the living room.

Her father read the newspaper, her mother was sitting next to Gillian in such a way that she couldn't look at her. Gillian looked at her mother's hands as she poured coffee, passed her a cup, took one herself, wizened hands too brown for the early season, with age spots and half a dozen rings on her fingers. As a young woman, her mother had been beautiful. Gillian wondered how she coped with the loss of her beauty, and if it was easier when it happened gradually and not just like that. She had read somewhere that most people had a completely false self-image, thinking of themselves as slimmer, younger, and more attractive than they really were. Perhaps to herself her mother was still the beautiful young woman in her wedding picture that stood on the sideboard. Certainly, she still looked after herself, but the futility of her efforts only made her decline sadder.

You look like you've put on weight, said her mother.

Gillian stayed longer than she had meant to. She went out to the garden with her father, and he showed her a couple of bushes he had planted. Later on, all three of them were in the living room again, reading. Gillian went to lie on the bed in her old room. Her mother was in the kitchen, getting dinner ready. Her father wandered around, perhaps he was looking for something. The times Gillian had visited him in his workshop, he had been a different man altogether, full of energy, choleric, but often in a good mood and generous. Whereas at home, he resembled a wounded animal, looking for a place to hide.

And you're sure it's all right if we go skiing next week? her mother asked.

Oh, yes, said Gillian, it's not a dangerous operation. And you'll see my new face soon enough.

Then why don't you go somewhere, to the mountains or the sea? asked her mother. You've got time.

By myself? said Gillian, and carried the glasses into the living room.

She set the table. When she came back to the kitchen, her mother looked at her apprehensively, but Gillian didn't say anything else. After dinner, they watched the news.

I'd better go now, said Gillian.

Her parents made no effort to keep her. They saw her to the door, her mother hugged her, her father shook hands. Break a leg, eh, said Gillian, and climbed into her car. When she had turned, she looked at the house again. The door was shut.

That evening Gillian checked her e-mails, but there was nothing for Miss Julie.

The text Hubert sent her after showing her his pictures had offended Gillian. He had asked if she was disappointed. After that she didn't write for two weeks, and he hung back as well. Matthias asked her what the matter was, but she just shook her head and said she had a lot to do, half the editorial team was away on autumn breaks.

Finally she wrote him an e-mail that accused him of exploiting her. Not every woman you lure into your studio will strip for you.

Hubert answered at once, it was as though he had been waiting for her to write. He was friendly but provocatively calm, wrote that he hadn't asked her to model for him, though he admitted he had entertained the possibility. He had decided basically not to continue with the series of nudes and to start on something new, but **it might** be interesting to have one last go. It would be different anyway, he wrote, seeing as you're not a complete stranger to me, and I wouldn't want to photograph you but paint you from life. Might you be interested?

What happens with the picture? asked Gillian without a salutation or greeting.

I'll give it to you, replied Hubert.

I can hardly come home with a nude painting of myself, wrote Gillian. He wrote: I wasn't thinking in terms of a nude.

Unusually, the program was wrapped on a Monday, and Gillian got Tuesday off. When she woke up, Matthias was standing by the window, a cup of coffee in his hand.

Look at the fog, he said, you're lucky.

No sooner was he gone than she showered and dressed. She tried to imagine the picture Hubert would paint of her. In his last e-mail he had asked her to wear a dress. She spent a long time in front of her wardrobe. Finally she decided on a classical high-necked chiffon dress that Matthias liked. She put on a pearl necklace and pearl earrings he had given her for their engagement. She didn't care for them, they made her seem old, but they seemed the right thing for an oil painting.

Now, by daylight and in fog, the area around Hubert's studio seemed even bleaker. Opposite the old textile mill was an ugly '80s office block with red metal cladding. It was a busy road. Outside the studio building stood a young man and an even younger woman, smoking. They took in

Gillian. The man was standing directly in front of the door and only moved aside at the very last moment.

Are you looking for someone? asked the young woman.

I've got an appointment, said Gillian, though the expression sounded a little absurd here.

The long passageway was dimly lit. Gillian walked down to the end, knocked on Hubert's door, and walked in without waiting to be admitted. Hubert had tidied up since the last time she'd been here. He had set up the easel in front of the sofa and put a big piece of chipboard on it.

Did you find the way all right? he asked casually and helped Gillian out of her coat. He looked at her. A dress without pleats would have been easier, technically speaking. How much time have you got?

Till midday, said Gillian.

He asked her to sit on the sofa, any way that was comfortable. No sooner had she sat down than he told her not to slump. He went up to her, laid his hand very gently on her shoulders, and pulled her upper body forward a little.

Is this all right?

When she nodded, he marked the position of her feet with red tape. Then he paced about the room in silence and looked at her from different angles. He put a film in his camera and took a few pictures.

Just to have something to fall back on, he said.

Finally, he moved the easel back from the sofa a little, marked its position with tape as well, and clipped a piece of packing paper to the board. Her position quickly became uncomfortable.

Is it all right if I take my shoes off?

Hubert nodded, and Gillian slipped off her pumps. After a while, her feet felt cold, and she put them on again.

Do you mind sitting still? asked Hubert. And don't smile. But no sooner had she changed her expression than he complained again. This isn't a photo shoot. Can't you just look normal? As if you were alone?

Gillian asked him if he was already working on her face.

It's your whole posture, he said. I can't see you if you're acting.

Gillian had been photographed many times, but it had always been a matter of playing a part, first in the theater, then in publicity shots. She struck a pose in front of the camera, got into positions she had seen in magazines. The best pictures were ones in which she could hardly recognize herself. Now that she wasn't allowed to move, she had no real sense of how Hubert was seeing her.

You have an enormous head, he said matter-of-factly. He unclipped the sketch, let it fall to the floor, and put up a new piece of packing paper on the backboard. After three-quarters of an hour they took a break.

Can I have a look? asked Gillian.

Sure, said Hubert, as he took an old espresso can apart. Do you want coffee?

Marked on the paper in charcoal she could see the shape of the room and the furniture. Her body was roughly sketched but it looked astonishingly lifelike. Even so, she wasn't satisfied. She had hoped the picture would tell her something new.

I wonder what you're going to discover in me, she said to Hubert, who had filled the espresso can and put it on the hot plate.

I don't see anything in you. I'll be pleased if I manage the exterior half decently.

Gillian knelt on the floor and leafed through the sketches. Hubert brought two full cups of espresso. He stopped just in front of her and said, stay like that. He set the cups on the floor, got a big sketchbook off a shelf, and started drawing her in quick strokes. By the time Gillian was allowed her coffee, it had gone cold.

Maybe it's better if you're standing up. He drank his coffee all in one go, left the dirty cups in the sink, and clipped a fresh piece of paper on the board.

They tried out all sorts of poses that morning: Gillian sitting on a chair, standing behind the chair leaning against the back, looking at Hubert, looking out the window, with her back to him or sideways. Sometimes he just looked at her without drawing her. Sometimes he took one or two photos. The poses tired Gillian, but she enjoyed the atmosphere of concentration, the attention Hubert gave her, and the gentle touches with which he coaxed her into different positions. By the time it was twelve and she had to go, there was a whole heap of sketches on the floor next to the easel.

Tomorrow the same time? asked Hubert. And please be sure to wear something different.

When Gillian arrived in the studio the next morning, the previous day's sketches were taped up on the wall. Again, Hubert helped her out of her coat. She wore a tightly fitting short skirt, sleeveless top, and dark stockings.

He had decided on a pose overnight. He set Gillian in an uncomfortable straight-backed cane chair and asked her to cross her arms. He took her right hand and put it on her left knee, and put the left on her right thigh.

Sit up straight, he said. How does that feel?

Not comfortable, said Gillian. Any chance of a cushion?

Hubert shook his head. We mustn't let you be too comfortable, otherwise you'll get that self-satisfied look on your face again.

This position feels stupid, said Gillian. I'd never sit like this.

So much the better, he said. Before he began, he set an egg timer for forty-five minutes. When it goes off, we can have a break, he said.

He went up to Gillian again and tweaked her clothes. He hardly spoke while drawing, but his facial expression changed continually, sometimes he looked angry, then suddenly he brightened. He drew his eyebrows together, looked intensely focused for a while, then relaxed again. Gillian looked out the window, where there was a huge mound of gravel, presumably spoils from some sort of dig. Behind it was a wooded slope. The sky was overcast. In spite of the uncomfortable position, Gillian's thoughts started to wander, as though the cramped attitude evoked certain memories. She thought about her early days at drama school, her strickenness when the teacher had criticized her. You're acting—that was his refrain—be yourself, show yourself. Only when she was completely exhausted, despairing and close to tears, did the teacher sometimes say, now that was the real you. Just for a moment.

Gillian was jolted out of her memories when Hubert asked her to please concentrate.

What does that mean? She asked. I thought as far as you're concerned I might as well be a milk jug or a bowl of fruit.

A jug doesn't look out the window, he said. You're dissolving.

When the egg timer rang, they took a short break. Gillian went to the bathroom, which was at the other end of the passageway. It was dirty, and even though the window was open and it was freezing cold in the tiny space, the stink was sickening. When she returned to the studio, Hubert had replaced the board with a prepared canvas and was in the process of mixing colors and getting brushes lined up. She walked up and down the room, stretching her legs.

All ready? he asked finally and wound the egg timer again.

She sat down. He adjusted her attitude and ran his hand over her hair to smooth it. Gillian settled down to watch Hubert paint. He had the brush out, and to judge by his sweeping movements he was painting the outlines.

It comes and goes, he said. Painting from photographs is definitely easier. Then he stopped talking; a little later he swore. It's not possible to render a three-dimensional object on a flat canvas.

By the object do you mean me? asked Gillian.

I don't even know what makes people try, he said, ignoring her. I only know I can't paint what I see. It would be better just to look at people instead of painting pictures of them.

So why do you do it?

He groaned.

Gillian imagined a museum with empty walls. People walked through the rooms, stopped in front of one another, took a step back, circled and scrutinized each other.

Hubert snapped his fingers. Hello? Anyone home?

The worst were the first few minutes after each break. Each time Gillian would think she couldn't possibly hold her pose for another forty-five minutes. Her mouth was dry, she needed to clear her throat, somewhere she had an itch that she would give anything to scratch. As time passed, she got used to sitting still. She still felt the pain in her back and bottom, but it had become part of her. She became stiller, stopped wondering what she would look like in the picture and who would get to see it. The painting would exist independently of her, it wasn't a copy, not a depiction. Every snapshot would contain more of her than this painting. The next time the egg timer went off, she walked around next to Hubert and looked at what he had done.

If you want, she said, you can paint me naked.

For two days Gillian had been going around with the proofs of the second book by a rising young novelist. She had taken the train out to Hubert's studio and had read another dozen pages. When she looked down at her cell phone during one of the breaks, she saw that her editor had sent her a text, asking if the book was worth devoting a slot to, and if she had an idea for how to do it. It wasn't easy for books to get coverage, you couldn't get interesting images out of writers. Think outside the box, the series editor said every time, I don't want to see another shot of a moody author tramping through autumn leaves. Gillian wrote back to say she wasn't far enough along yet, but she'd know by tomorrow. After dinner, she went on reading the proofs and wondering how the young author could be produced for television. She was glad of the distraction. At eleven Matthias came into her office and said he was going to bed. By midnight she had roughed out a concept for a film, no walk in the woods but a retelling of the novel with some archive footage, and a brief interview with the author on the difficulties of a second novel, and a couple of clips from a reading, with comments from readers. That should stand a chance in the editorial meeting. She went to the bathroom and got undressed. She looked at herself in the mirror for a long time. She turned and looked over her shoulder.

Normally, Thursdays weren't too strenuous, but Gillian spent almost the whole morning editing a piece. In the afternoon it was okayed, and she made a couple of phone calls to advance the concept she wanted to present in the editorial meeting tomorrow. She still hadn't gotten to the end of the book. It was an eccentric story with lots of humorous inserts, but even so—or maybe just because—she was bored by it. If you asked her, most literary publications were superfluous anyway. Perhaps it was her fault, but it was more and more unusual for her to be caught up in a book. When writers complained that they were never invited to be on the program, she often felt tempted to say, write better books.

She was already thinking of canceling the proposal, but when she met her boss by the coffee machine he said he was looking forward to hearing from her. She went home at three. She read a bit more of the proofs, but she couldn't concentrate. She had told Matthias at breakfast that she was going to see Dagmar that evening.

When she set off a little before six, it was raining gently, and it felt colder than in the morning. She looked at the other passengers in the streetcar and tried to imagine them naked. Old women, businesspeople, mothers who had collected their little ones from day care—all naked. A young, smartly dressed businessman whose upper body was densely haired, a man with such a big belly that you couldn't see his penis, a big-breasted woman, a young woman with thin reddish pubic hair and a genital piercing. Pleats of skin, wrinkles, light and dark skin, spots, freckles, and moles. Gillian felt reminded of medieval pictures of the Day of Judgment, tiny little people doubled over with pain and guilt. She tried to remember the name of the painter who had persuaded hundreds of people to take off their clothes for him and all lie down on the ground.

She had to change at the central station. The big hall was full of people. Gillian wriggled through, the proximity of so many others was suddenly disagreeable to her. During the train ride, she remained standing by the door.

By the time she got there, it was almost dark. She hadn't taken an umbrella, and her face and hair were wet as she strode quickly down the passageway of the studio building. She walked in without knocking. Hubert was on the sofa, reading the newspaper, beside him on the floor was a bottle of beer. He put the newspaper away and looked up at her. She dropped her coat on the sofa beside him. He looked apathetic. He got up and kissed her on both cheeks.

Are you ready?

Gillian stooped to pick up the beer bottle, took a long drink, and set it back on the floor. She looked at him and nodded. Hubert said she could leave her things on the sofa and went over to the easel to fix the backboard.

The floor's not very clean I'm afraid, he said with his back to her. Sorry.

In front of the easel stood the empty chair that Gillian had sat in yesterday, with a small electric heater by it.

She pulled her sweater over her head with both hands. Underneath she had on a sleeveless linen blouse. She undid the top two buttons, hesitated briefly. All the time she hadn't taken her eyes off Hubert. He stood in front of the easel, turned away from her, busying himself with his sketching things. Even so, she turned her back on him when unbuttoning her jeans. They were quite tight, and she had to wriggle to get them off. She thought how silly that must look. She took off her thin kneesocks, and undid the rest of the buttons on her blouse. Then she asked Hubert for a hanger. At that stage he had to turn round, but he kept his eyes on her face.

Linen creases so easily, she said, smiling, when he passed her a wire hanger.

Now she had the feeling that the situation was under control. In her underwear she sat down on the chair.

Do you want me to sit like yesterday?

I thought . . . , Hubert began, but he didn't finish the sentence.

Gillian stood up, turned away, and quickly took off her bra and underpants. When she walked naked through the room, she moved differently than usual, slower and more

erect, a little stiffly. She was sure that Hubert was watch
ing her now. The thought that he had already seen and
painted so many women naked unsettled her. She folded
her underwear under the other things on the sofa and sat
down on the chair in front of the easel.

Do you like what you see, then? she asked, and right
away was furious with herself.

Hubert didn't reply. She had taken the same position as
the day before and was happy at the way her crossed arms
were shielding her. Hubert walked around for a while, and
then very slowly approached her, repeatedly stopping to
look at her. She tried to sense what was in his mind, his
expression was serious and intent.

Do you mind if I take some photographs?

Gillian hesitated, then nodded.

He clicked in a roll of film, then went in very close with
the camera. He seemed to have more courage when he was
able to hide behind the equipment. When the film had
been shot off, he put it in an envelope and sealed it. Then
at last he started sketching.

The cane seat cut into her bottom, and the electric
heater only warmed one side of her body. She tried to
think of something else. She asked herself what she was
doing there. If Matthias saw the painting, he was certain
to make a huge scene. Of course he would recognize her,
whatever Hubert said. And he would never believe that she
hadn't slept with the painter. He knew her past, for ten
years after drama school she had done pretty much whatever she felt like doing. Sometimes she had slept with a
man purely because she admired his lifestyle or because
she wanted to know what it would feel like to deceive her

boyfriend of the time. Matthias often quizzed her about those years, and she didn't keep anything from him. Well, you're mine now, she had often heard that sentence from him, and even though she didn't much like the expression, it did give her a kind of security. She had no reason to play around now. If she did, and he found out, that would be the end of everything, of that she was certain. She couldn't account for what it was about Hubert that attracted her. He dressed scruffily and didn't seem to be interested in his appearance. And his laconic, even grouchy manner was enough to lead Gillian to expect coarseness or inattentiveness. She had had a brief relationship with a painter once before, and that had been a disaster. Perhaps she was in search of uncertainty, in the hope of being unsettled. She needed perhaps to be made to feel who she was. That sounded like something that would be more at home in a self-help book. Sometimes she and Matthias had giggled over the tips in magazines, techniques to keep a tired relationship alive, and even so he arranged for them to spend holidays in a spa hotel in the mountains where they would be pampered with massages and baths and good food. Then they slept together, as though that too was on the menu. Currently, Gillian found sex with him less satisfying than the fact that they had it at all. It was proof that their relationship was in good shape, and that things could go on as they were.

The egg timer went off. Her pose had come to feel like a protective garment, but as soon as she got up she felt her nudity again. Even so, she walked over to Hubert who still had the charcoal in his hand. He took a step back to inspect the drawing, quite as though not to be too close to her. He was more careful of her altogether since she was naked. She turned to him, stood next to the drawing, and copied the uncertain expression on the girl's face.

Did I really look like that?

She tried a big confident smile, but it didn't come off. Hubert went over to the door and took down a thin kimono from the hook and passed it to her.

I don't want to be responsible for your catching cold.

She looked at the sketch. Even though it was just a rough sketch, she could see the likeness, but it didn't strike her as significant.

Are you happy with it? she asked.

Hubert shook his head. I get the feeling there's nothing coming from you, he said. A bit of shyness at the start, but after that you were just gone.

What do you expect from me? I've never done this before.

Presence. You've got to be here so that something can happen between us.

Gillian smirked.

Get undressed, he said. Stand here. Feet apart. So that you feel solidly rooted. Do you feel the floor? Your weight?

Gillian recalled the exercises in her first year of drama school, even then she hadn't quite understood what they meant by presence. Hubert circled around her at a distance, stopped still behind her. She could feel his attentiveness.

What are you thinking about?

I was remembering drama school.

How do you feel?

I don't know. Tired.

Sit down.

She had to sit on the cold floor, her knees drawn up, arms on her knees, one hand grasping her other wrist. She thought of a statue by Aristide Maillol in exactly that pose. Hubert wound up the egg timer, started drawing. Sometimes he groaned loudly, or hurled the charcoal on the floor. It's not working. The timer went off, they split a beer, a new pose. The more it went on, the more taciturn Hubert grew. Sometimes he would crumple up a sheet of paper after a single line. Gillian was tired, her body cramped, she was hurting. In the next break, she did a couple of stretches, but Hubert had already wound the clock again.

Get undressed.

She opened the kimono. He stepped up behind her and almost ripped it off her.

Lie down.

She lay on her front, her head pillowed on her folded arms. She could feel herself getting goose pimples all over.

I need to go to the bathroom.

Not now. Arms down by your sides.

The cold floor pressed against her cheekbones. Hubert stood close beside her, she could only see his feet and legs.

Lie on your back.

When Gillian turned over, bits of grit were clinging to her belly, her breasts, her face. Chill from the floor crept into her, her breasts rose and fell. She covered her pudenda with her hand.

No, said Hubert.

She took her hand away. Slowly she calmed down. She lay there like a corpse. Hubert was still standing very close to her, looking down. She studied the ceiling, the electric wires that led to the ugly halogen lamps. Dirty gray shadows had formed around the lamps. She tried to look Hubert in the eye. After he finally returned her look, he walked away. She sat up and saw him standing at the window, staring out into the dark. Gillian stood up, and with her hands brushed the dirt off her face and body. Then she picked up the kimono off the floor and went over to Hubert.

I'm sorry.

It doesn't matter.

She pressed herself against him, placed her hands on his chest. When he still didn't react, she undid the belt of the kimono.

It's all right, she said.

Her voice sounded false, she was speaking lines from a script. She started stroking his neck and shoulder, her breath came faster, she kept her mouth close to his ear. She wanted to be aroused, wanted him to. He broke away with a jerk and took a step to the side, without turning to face her.

Stop that!

For a long time neither spoke.

Don't you fancy me?

Finally Hubert turned toward her and looked at her.

My girlfriend's having a baby. The due date's next month.

Gillian laughed and took a step toward him.

Who cares, we're grown-ups.

She was playing a part in a bad film. Even so, her lust was genuine. She wanted him to grab her and push her onto the sofa. It would be like a punishment that would relieve her. Just then the egg timer went off. It seemed not to want to stop. Hubert went to the door and opened it.

Please go.

Gillian's father stood by the window, even though there was nothing to be seen anymore besides the doctors' parking spaces, a bit of lawn, and some small detached houses. In the past few days Gillian had often stood at that same window and asked herself who lived in those houses and what sort of lives were conducted in the rhythm of the lamps going on and off, behind the opening and closing curtains, whose shadows were flitting over the blinds. But her father wasn't looking out, his head was lowered. He had hardly been there for fifteen minutes, and already he was restless. One of the nurses had taken off the bandage so that he could see his daughter's face.

Gillian stepped behind him and stopped a couple of paces away. He had driven down from the mountains and interrupted his skiing holiday expressly for her sake. She was touched, but when she tried to say so, he gestured dismissively, it hadn't even taken him three hours.

The doctors have done a good job, he said. It's looking all right, almost like before.

Gillian looked nothing like before. Now that she could identify her features again, she saw even more clearly how she had changed. She would never look the way she had before the accident.

I had a word with the doctor, said her father, after the third operation there'll be hardly any trace left.

That's in five months, said Gillian. In summer.

81

She had called her boss after the operation. He had suggested expanding her editorial function, since she wasn't able to appear in front of the camera for now. He had cautiously felt her out about the prognosis for her face. In five months it's supposed to be fully restored, said Gillian, with the help of a bit of makeup. Let's talk nearer the time, said her boss. When can you start work?

When can you start work? asked her father.

He had never liked her job, never even approved of drama lessons. She was surprised to see him at her graduation show. Nor was her father impressed with her journalistic training. For him, journalists were all lefties, out to wreck the private sector. As a student Gillian had started presenting a lifestyle show for a local television station. She had been so good at it that she was called in for a screen test when the national broadcaster was looking for a host for a new flagship arts program. But even after Gillian started getting more and more prominence, her father continued to criticize her profession. The thing that most got on his nerves was when a customer or acquaintance of his asked if he was related to her, and he had to undergo a detailed commentary on the program and what she was wearing and what the magazines had to say about it.

After the accident a tabloid newspaper published a blurred hospital picture of her. Her father had pulled the page from his briefcase and held it out to her. He said no one could account for the picture, presumably it had been taken by someone working here, who had sold it to the paper. Gillian was barely recognizable, it must have been taken by a cell phone camera and with poor light. Under the picture was a brief report: tragic accident and so forth. She didn't feel like reading the piece. Instead she looked at the other picture, of her and Matthias, taken at some party or other, her smile appeared forced, and she looked older than she was.

What am I supposed to do? she asked. It could have been almost anyone.

She passed the paper back to her father, and he returned it to his briefcase. She thought he would say that's your comeuppance, but all he said was that he had lodged a complaint with the hospital management and telephoned the paper. He had even talked to his lawyer, but the lawyer wasn't interested. She was of public interest, it made it difficult to defend her privacy. If you shared your happiness with journalists, you shouldn't be surprised if they were interested in your misfortune as well.

When are you starting again? asked her father.

That's finished, said Gillian. You won't have to be angry with them anymore now. I'm not going back into editorial to receive anyone's sympathy.

She didn't feel like writing scripts for Maia, who, thanks to her accident, was getting the chance to move from her desk to in front of the camera.

What will you do instead? asked her father.

She couldn't tell from his tone if he was relieved or concerned.

I don't know yet, she said, something will turn up.

Do you want the use of the holiday house for a while? he asked. We won't be there past Sunday.

Neither of them mentioned that she and Matthias had been going to spend the next week in the mountains.

On the first floor was the maternity ward. In the elevator was a list of the babies born during the past few days. When Gillian went down to the kiosk in the entrance hall for cigarettes or a newspaper, she would see the young couples standing around with their new babies. They looked lost, as though they were waiting for someone to come by and say something complimentary. Behind their smiles Gillian saw panic in the face of the horrifying creature they had made, and for which they were now responsible, without really knowing what they were going to do. She felt them avoiding her eye.

It was a sunny day in February, the air was cool, and the wind chased the occasional cloud across the sky. Gillian stood on the balcony of her room, smoking. She had wrapped herself in a blanket and was looking down at the city and the lake. She felt chilly as she lit another cigarette. Smoking was banned everywhere in the hospital and a nurse passing by outside made an indignant face and wafted her hand in front of her face. Gillian ignored her. A young couple left the building. The man carried the baby awkwardly under his arm. The woman had linked arms with him, she walked a little uncertainly, and didn't look particularly pleased. Suddenly the w-word made an appearance, I am a widow, and it was more shocking than her injury, than Matthias's death, than anything.

The clouds suddenly gave way to the sun and, dazzled, Gillian took a backward step. The doctor came in to say goodbye. He said she shouldn't go out in the sun for the time being and should avoid getting her face wet for a few days. Also she shouldn't take any exercise, and should avoid all forms of exertion. Apart from that, she could please herself. He shook hands with Gillian and said he had to go, they would see each other again in five months' time. Gillian looked at her watch. It was a little after two. She packed her case and went out into the corridor. She quickly said goodbye to the nurses. Something kept her from walking out of the main hospital exit. At the end of the landing was a staircase that went down to the emergency ward and a side exit. She called a taxi. While she waited, she wondered where she would go. She didn't want to see any of her friends, no one she had known from before, who would compare her old face to the new one. When the taxi finally arrived, she put on her dark glasses and almost ran the few steps to it.

From home, she called the police station and asked to speak to Frau Bauer. She was away from her desk, but the man took a note of Gillian's number and promised his colleague would get back to her. When she phoned three hours later, Gillian was almost in tears. She reminded the policewoman who she was.

What can I do for you?

Gillian hesitated, then she said, my husband wasn't to blame for the accident. I was supposed to drive us home. And then I got drunk and I couldn't.

You told me that already, said the policewoman.

It wasn't his fault, said Gillian again, and by now she was crying.

He still shouldn't have been driving, said the policewoman coolly. Perhaps you do need help. Shall I give you that victims' support number again?

I'm not the victim, said Gillian and hung up.

She called Matthias's mother and told her everything, but she wouldn't hear of Gillian's guilt either. She said there was no point in looking for a guilty party. Matthias's death had been God's will. The conversation was over almost as quickly as that with the policewoman.

Over the next few days, Gillian kept thinking of the New Year's party and of how the accident might have been avoided. She should have insisted on staying the night at Dagmar's, she shouldn't have gotten into the car, she should never have allowed Hubert to take photographs of her nude.

Early on Sunday she called her parents at the vacation house. Her father picked up. She asked him where exactly the accident had happened. Someone from his workshop had picked up the totaled vehicle, and he was able to tell her the place. Gillian said she was happy to take his offer of staying in the house for a while. He said they wouldn't be leaving till tonight, the weather was fine, and they wanted to get another day's skiing in.

What about coming up today? It would be good to see you there.

I can't manage that, she said.

Well, you know where we keep the keys, said her father.

She spent Sunday straightening up the apartment and packing a suitcase, though she didn't know how long she would be staying in the mountains. On Monday morning she drove to the scene of the crash. She parked by a forest path a hundred yards farther on and went back on foot. By the side of the road was a withered bouquet of flowers with a burned-down votive candle, the only clue that there had been an accident here. Gillian wondered who had put it there. She picked it up and put it on her backseat. When she stopped at a rest stop an hour later, to fill up, she threw it in a trash can that had *Thank You* written on it in four languages.

Never will I succeed in putting as much strength in a portrait as there is in a head. The mere fact of living demands such willpower and energy...

ALBERTO GIACOMETTI

Dust was time in material form, Hubert could no longer remember who had said it, or where he had read it. At any rate, a lot of time seemed to have collected in his studio, because there was a thin, almost transparent layer of dust over everything. He didn't bother to wipe it away, he had only come to take a look through his old stuff and see if there was anything he could use. The big nudes, the naked housewife series, as his gallerist called them, he didn't even look at, they had become so strange to him, it was as though they were by someone else. He took a stack of large folders from a shelf and opened them one after the other, industrial landscapes, pencil drawings of machinery, portraits, and nudes, the oldest things dated back to his student days. After briefly hesitating, he took down a folder labeled *Astrid*. It contained two dozen photographs and a few sketches. He had done them right at the beginning of their relationship, during a summer holiday in the south of France. They had driven around, staying in campsites. In every picture there was Astrid naked in a different landscape, sometimes so small that she could hardly be made out. He had thought of drawing the whole series in crayon but only finished a very few. In his memory they had been better than they were.

He put them all back in the folder and went on to the next one.

An hour later, Hubert was back outside the building. He had managed to find nothing usable, but carted the slides and projector into his car anyway, raw material that sometime might come in handy. It was midnight, but the air was balmy.

He had been teaching at the art school for six years now. There were two weeks left of the semester, but he was already finished, and he felt that strange mix of freedom and what now? that he was caught up in every summer.

He had lit a cigarette and rolled the window down. There were still plenty of people around, in the distance he heard a police siren. All month, the weather had been unusually warm and dry. First, Hubert had been pleased about it, then the longer it went on, the more it disquieted him. The news carried reports of desiccated crops, and everyone was talking about climate change, but that wasn't the cause of his disquiet. When he drove over the bridge, he saw the lakeside lights flashing a storm warning.

The next morning a light rain was falling. Hubert had opened the window, and a cool wind blew in his face. He had gotten up early and prepared the apartment for a few months without him. On the car radio he listened to the weather forecast. It seemed the next few days would remain cold and rainy, and the snow line would fall below a thousand meters.

He got caught up in the rush-hour traffic. He wasn't a very experienced driver, and when he abruptly changed lanes, or got moving too late after the lights turned, the cars behind him honked. On the Autobahn other cars sat on his tail. After two hours, just before he exited the Autobahn, he stopped at a rest site and drank a cup of coffee. In the restaurant there were some pictures by a painter who had made a name for himself depicting elephants and tigers. A little leaflet was provided, which listed the absurdly high prices that were charged for the works. Hubert was almost physically disgusted by the paintings, and he soon set off.

Driving on, he briefly entertained the thought of making a living like that artist. Since he'd begun teaching, he hardly got around to painting anymore. He persuaded himself that it was because he was pushed for time. In his younger days, he always used to mock artists who feathered their nests as professors, but following Lukas's birth he accepted an offer from the college. A regular job seemed to be the only way of having a reasonably comfortable middle-class life and not ending up as an impoverished artist in the gutter.

When Lukas started kindergarten, Astrid went back to work in the property department of the same bank where she had worked before. They moved into the town next door, where they managed to buy a small house on the edge of the fields.

As well as her work, Astrid pursued her interest in energy and the body. Hubert wasn't impressed by the esoteric life-help scene she started to move in. He passed

occasional ironic remarks, to which she reacted so vio
lently that he didn't say anything the next time she regis-
tered for a weekend course in psychodrama or breathing
therapy.

After a short while, she began to offer special coaching for entrepreneurs. She converted their basement into
a sort of treatment room. On the walls she hung pictures
by an Italian woman artist Hubert knew. The multiply
exposed cityscapes through which anonymous individu-
als moved had always struck him as being on the cool side,
but Astrid said no, they were perfect for her clientele. On
a little corner table she put a rose quartz. She got a flyer
printed up, full of executives and problem awareness,
resources and parameters, and before long the first clients
arrived, usually big shots from her bank, and disappeared
downstairs with her.

When I have a large enough customer base I mean to go
full-time, said Astrid over dinner.

She got terribly angry when Hubert said the only reason her bosses came to her for coaching was that she was
so good-looking. Or is it an accident that you always seem
to be in short skirts for your sessions?

You need to think about your own life-work balance,
she countered. It would be a start if you weren't always
mowing the lawn when I have clients.

In objective terms, they were doing very well, but Hubert
felt increasingly like an impostor when he stood in front of
his students and critiqued their work. He always had something big planned for the holidays and then kept putting it

off, doing odd jobs about the house and garden or busying himself with vague research for projects that were never realized. He read a lot, and he saw colleagues. He still kept his studio in the old textile mill, but he rarely went there anymore. At first he had supposed his difficulties marked the beginning of a new productive phase. He put off his gallerist month after month. And he in turn asked less and less about what Hubert was working on now and instead sent him photos of the dog he had acquired and invitations to the openings of other artists in his stable. Hubert took a quick look at the postcards and laid them aside with a mixture of envy and irritation at the ardor with which his colleagues pursued their humdrum ideas.

Then one day he got an e-mail from Arno, the head of a cultural center in the mountains where he had had his first and only large solo exhibition seven years before. To him it all seemed incredibly remote, and he had no significant memory of the place, the rooms or the people there, but this Arno guy still seemed to be full of their meeting. He addressed him by his first name, wrote enthusiastically about that show, and invited Hubert to come back. He gave him a budget and carte blanche, he could stay in the cultural center as long as he wanted, only the date for the exhibition was set, the end of June next year. Hubert felt like turning it down immediately, but then he printed out the e-mail and left it with a pile of other stuff in his in-box.

After dinner, he told Astrid about the invitation from Arno. That was a nice time, she said, do you remember?

I helped you hang the paintings. I was pregnant then. We had this little room right at the top of the building with a creaky bed. Arno once made some remark about it, but you weren't bothered. She smiled quickly, then her face took on an expression as though she was confused by what she remembered. Could be, said Hubert, who could remember nothing of all this.

They had been sitting in the garden, Lukas was playing in the meadow with a neighbor's son. Hubert collected the dirty dishes and carried them into the kitchen. He was barefoot and felt the chill of the grass at approaching nightfall. When he came back, Astrid asked him why he didn't want to accept the invitation.

Because I've got nothing to show, he said.

It doesn't get any easier, she said. Sometime you'll need to start working again. The scenery up there is beautiful.

Beautiful landscapes are no use for good paintings.

There are lots of radionic power places around there.

That's more your thing. Are you trying to get rid of me, by any chance?

Astrid got up and called Lukas. Her voice sounded strangely rough when she told him to come home right away. Ten minutes later, she came out into the garden and said Lukas wanted his good night kiss from his father.

It was cool inside, all the blinds were down. Lukas lay perfectly still in his bed, waiting. At such times Hubert thought of him as a strange creature whose world was so much bigger and darker than his own. Hubert bent down, only for Lukas to grab him around the neck and start kissing him frantically on both cheeks.

Enough, enough, said Hubert. You go to sleep now.

As he walked over to the stairs, he remembered an early cycle of pictures, little colored pencil drawings of kitchens, bedrooms, and living rooms. There were no people in them, but you could sense that someone had either just left or was just about to arrive. He stopped on the top step. From the kitchen he could hear the clatter of dishes. Then he saw Astrid walking through the dark corridor, without noticing him up on the stair. She was carrying a wine bottle and two glasses. Her walk looked as though she was trying not to be noticed. Hubert went softly down the stairs and saw that Astrid had stopped at the glass door that led out into the garden. She was hesitating, perhaps she had heard something or seen something. He took a couple of rapid steps toward her, put his arm around her waist, and kissed her neck. She turned to face him. When he made to kiss her again, she freed herself.

I need to talk to you.

Hubert could only dimly remember the conversation. On the next-door property a halogen beam had come on every other minute or so, because some animal had triggered the motion sensor. In the distance, there was the quiet drone of traffic on the Autobahn. It had gotten colder. Astrid had long since bundled herself up in a blanket. When they finally went in at around midnight, Hubert had trouble walking in a straight line. He carried in two empty wine bottles, set them on the dining table, and lay down on the sofa. Astrid went up to bed without a word.

It was the first of many conversations that always took the same course. Astrid said she felt trapped in their relationship. It was so different with Rolf. He opened up to her. Ever since she had started moving in the therapy scene, she spoke a new language.

Each time, she calmly explained her view of things to Hubert and reacted understandingly to his rage, which only made him still more furious. It all had nothing to do with him. Her decision had been made. In the end, Hubert had no alternative but to agree to a trial separation. Astrid was to stay in the house with Lukas, while he found a small apartment for himself.

Now that Hubert knew about Astrid's lover, she had no more reason to meet him clandestinely. Every second or third evening she went out. Then Hubert would sit at home all evening and watch Lukas, who had trouble sleeping and had awful nightmares when he did. When Astrid got back at one or whenever, Hubert was sitting in front of the TV, and she vanished upstairs without a word.

The semester was over in the middle of June, but Hubert still went in every day. He had taken a one-bedroom apartment near the lake. He had forgotten all about the invitation to the mountains when Arno sent him a reminder.

What do I have to do to convince you? he wrote. After lunch Hubert had coffee with the head of his department. She knew about his separation from Astrid and urged him to accept the invitation. It was almost twelve months off, in all that time he would surely think of something. Perhaps the pressure of a deadline was just what he needed.

After lunch, Hubert replied to Arno: He'd be happy to come.

In July he went away on vacation with Astrid and Lukas. They had rented the house just after Christmas. Hubert had offered to step down in place of Rolf, but Astrid said they weren't that far along yet. She had no problem going on holiday with Hubert anyway.

During their two weeks in Denmark, the weather stayed cool and rainy. Lukas was bored. They did all sorts of activities, visited a safari park, a maritime museum on a restored three-master, and a glassworks, where Lukas made a glass mold of his hand. At least by day Hubert could give himself to the illusion that they were still a family. Lukas too seemed to appreciate that they were all together again. Astrid received a string of text messages and at least once a day a phone call. Then she would go into another room or, if they were outside, take a few steps away. Hubert watched her in the distance. She was serious and if anything more irritable after these conversations than before.

When Lukas was tucked up in bed, he and Astrid would sit in the living room drinking wine and reading. Eventually Astrid would say she was tired and head for the bathroom. Hubert put his book down and listened to the unfamiliar noises of the strange house, the creaking of the steps, the whooshing of the pipes, and the wind that was always blowing here. He waited for half an hour, then he would go to the bathroom himself. They slept in separate rooms, except once, when Astrid got up to go to bed and she whispered to him: Are you coming? He followed her up the stairs. On the landing she took him by the hand and led him into her room.

The next morning, neither of them talked about what had happened in the night, but for the rest of the vacation, Hubert noticed that Astrid would link arms with him when they walked, or kiss him when he bought ice cream for her and Lukas. Sometimes he would shock himself by thinking that this was the last holiday they would have together.

Their closeness during the two-week vacation only served to distance them further from one another. Their relationship became increasingly pally, they barely quarreled anymore when they met. They compared schedules and talked about who would collect Lukas from school or day care, and who would have him over what weekend. Astrid asked if Hubert knew where the warranty for the coffee machine was or if he would fix the puncture in Lukas's bike tire. They talked about their work, and sometimes Astrid even talked about Rolf, and Hubert listened without interrupting.

There was plenty to do in the garden, and Hubert took it on. He avoided going into the house. Only when he needed some tools from the basement did he go inside. Lukas often came out, played in his vicinity and kept half an eye on him all the time. Sometimes Hubert asked him to fetch something, and he would jump up and run and get it, as if he too preferred that his father didn't set foot in the house.

Hubert increasingly got used to the new situation, but he still refused all contact with Rolf. As if to punish him for it, Astrid talked about her friend all the time. He had started his own career advice business. That was what he called it, but in actual fact it went far beyond that.

He works according to holistic principles, he intuits his way into his opposite number, and then he can practically go backward and forward on the temporal axis and give advice, very concrete advice.

Is he your lover or your guru? asked Hubert.

Neither, she said. When he spends the night here, he stays in the guest room.

After the beginning of the new semester, Hubert had hardly any time to think about the invitation to the mountains. There was less to do in the garden, and the only times he went by the house were to pick Lukas up for the weekend or to bring him back. He tried to find out from him what was going on between Rolf and his mother, asked what they talked about, what they did together, but Lukas didn't like to talk about that.

In the fall, Hubert organized an exhibition for his students, and no sooner was that over than the planning started for an artists' ball at the end of the semester. The work wasn't unwelcome to him. Since he was living on his own, he had a lot of time on his hands, especially in the evenings. Sometimes he went to the cinema or the theater. He rarely saw friends. After Lukas's birth he had lost contact with most people anyway.

In January, in the course of a weekend skiing with the department, he started an affair with one of his students. Nina was in her final semester, she was attractive and energetic. For two months they met once a week. They slept together, and then they would discuss their work. At Easter, Nina wanted to go into the mountains with him, but Hubert said no, he was spending the holiday with his son.

Then bring him, she said. I've got nothing against animals and children.

The idea of spending a weekend with Lukas and Nina seemed absurd to Hubert, and he said as much. There followed their first and only quarrel, at the end of which they went their separate ways.

One reason is always lots of reasons, said Nina before she left. The fact that he oversaw her work was something she could deal with apparently better than he could. I'm not angry with you, she said. We had a good time.

Hubert thought more and more about the show. When he accepted the invitation, he had thought he would come up with an idea in plenty of time. Now, with the deadline looming ever larger, he didn't feel so sure anymore. His head of department asked him once or twice what he had planned. He shrugged.

I might do something with youngsters, he said, or something about mountains or water.

Maybe being up there will turn you into a landscape painter. When do you go?

End of May, he said. For a month.

When he was half out the door, she called after him to say he should put some of his newer work up on his home page. He discussed the exhibition with Nina as well. They were sitting in a bar drinking beer.

There's a bear on the loose up there, isn't there? she said. Did you read about it? You could do something with teddy bears. Or with bear poop. Like that African guy who works with elephant dung.

Chris Ofili, said Hubert. And he's British. To hear you, everything sounds so easy.

You just think my ideas are crap, admit it, she said, and laughed.

Sometimes Hubert asked himself when his creative crisis had started. It hadn't happened suddenly, at some point he had noticed that he no longer got a kick out of painting and that he hadn't started anything new for months. Maybe it had something to do with Lukas. He and Astrid hadn't planned on having a kid, and he was in the middle of the preparations for his first solo show when he learned about the pregnancy. It was the first time his work had gotten any serious attention, an art magazine ran some of the pictures, there was even a report about him on TV. A few days after the opening, a lot of the pictures had been sold, even though his gallerist had set the prices far too high. At that time, he was spending more time in the studio than at home. The gallerist had said he could paint as many naked housewives as he wanted, he would sell them all. Hubert didn't like it when his gallerist called his paintings that. So that was a no go. And the pictures were starting to bore him as well. Technically they were no longer a challenge, maybe the newer ones were a little bit better than their predecessors, but they still lacked oomph.

Then the first e-mail came from Miss Julie. Hubert had set up his home page a couple of years previously, but no one had ever written to him there. Her praise flattered him. She asked him about his influences, his methods, why he always painted naked women. He wrote back that he wasn't obsessed with women, it was just a subject cycle. Basically his pictures of women were a logical continuation of his empty room series before. Julie didn't believe him.

He didn't tell her about his girlfriend, or the child they were expecting. He didn't ask her about her circumstances either. Their e-mails were never entirely serious, Julie's especially were more playful than inquisitive. Hubert got a clearer sense of her, he was almost certain he would recognize her if they ever met.

When Julie asked him if he would paint her, his first thought was that she was just playing games again. He hesitated and asked her for a photo, but he wasn't unhappy when she didn't send him one. He had noticed he was spending all his energy on the exchange and thought perhaps he could invest that concentration in his work and get over the apathy that had been bothering him for months. No one else interested him.

A couple of days later he and Julie had met. When he saw Gillian sitting in the café, he wasn't surprised. He had been familiar with her face from her television show for a long time, but it was only when they met in the studio that he had felt her uncertainty and curiosity, which weren't so evident on the screen. He invited her back to his studio. While he was showing her his pictures, Gillian touched his hand, and he was this close to throwing his arm around her shoulder. He offered her a beer and watched her drink it. He saw the possibilities of her face, not so much its beauty as its variety, the many faces that were contained in it.

After Gillian had left, Hubert looked at the pictures he had taken of Astrid in the south of France again. He could remember their excitement when he stopped the car in the middle of the country road. Astrid got undressed in the car, while he looked around nervously. She tiptoed out on the pebbly ground, he framed the picture and took a shot. Once they were chased off by a farmer, another time Astrid got a thorn in her foot and they had to go to see a doctor. Astrid's poses were classical, and in their stiffness there was almost something cubist about the pictures. In drawing from the photographs, he had given more care to the landscape than to her body. After that she hadn't wanted to model for him anymore. One of the pictures had hung in their apartment for a while. Only when Hubert noticed how many of their visitors were embarrassed by it had he taken it down. Astrid hadn't said anything. Then he had started painting the small-format interiors. The fact that there were no people in them wasn't a concept, just lack of proficiency on his part.

The idea with the female passersby had occurred to

mini long before he ever told Astrid about it. You'd never get anyone to go along with that anyway, she said.

And at the beginning, it was true, no one had. Over time, Hubert got used to the refusals. From the way the women hesitated before rejecting him, he learned to see which ones he had a better chance with and how best to proceed. He left the city center and hung around the outskirts. The first time a woman consented was a rainy morning in spring. He stood outside a swimming pool and addressed a fit-looking woman of fifty or so, with short hair. When he had put his question to her, she laughed out loud and asked how could she be sure he wasn't a pervert. He said she couldn't, she would just have to trust him. He accompanied her back to her apartment. He was so excited that even while he was taking the photographs, he knew the pictures wouldn't come to anything. Still, he used up four or five rolls of film before thanking her and saying he had what he needed. Hubert promised to send her an invitation to the opening, if there should be one. The woman had actually come, along with her husband, and had been disappointed not to see herself in any of the paintings.

With each new model, Hubert got a little calmer, and the pictures a little better. Eventually, the sessions became predictable, and he noticed he was beginning to get bored. This was shortly before the exhibition, and even as the pictures were praised and he spouted nonsense about them in interviews, he already knew that he would have to get going on something else. His gallerist told him about a series of paintings by an American artist who for fifteen years had painted the same woman, a neighbor. He hadn't shown the pictures to anyone, not even his own wife or the woman's husband had known about them. Hubert got hold of a catalog of the pictures and decided to concentrate on a single model. When Gillian visited him in his studio, he thought she might be the one.

The idea of painting Gillian didn't let him go. As he went through the motions of completing his latest nude, he imagined how he would capture on canvas what he had seen in her face. Two weeks later she called. He disregarded the annoyance in her e-mails, he felt certain she was just as determined as he was. But the sessions went badly from the very beginning. Gillian had evidently imagined he would paint a portrait of her that she could put up on the wall at home, whereas he had no interest in just one picture. He had thought her presence would shape his paintings. He was on the point of throwing in the towel when she suggested posing for him naked. It wasn't so much her nakedness that interested him as the hope that she might be unsettled by it. But it didn't get any better. She struck attitudes. He had always left his models the freedom to be as they were, to make themselves comfortable. Gillian he forced into a pose that wasn't her, really as a last desperate attempt to undermine her. But even that hadn't worked, and he had given up.

Shortly after, Lukas was born. Once when Hubert took him to the pediatrician, he was leafing through magazines in a waiting room and ran into a short report on Gillian's accident. He tried several times to write her an e-mail, but he couldn't find the right words and gave up.

The next time he was in the studio, several weeks later, he took the sketches of her off the walls.

Before setting off for the mountains, Hubert packed his outdoor gear he hadn't used in twenty years and bought new hiking shoes and a waterproof. He was going on Monday. The weekend before, he had Lukas with him. They went to the zoo, and Hubert made pancakes, Lukas's favorite. On Sunday he dropped him off a little earlier than usual. Astrid asked if he had time for coffee. While she put on water to boil, he looked at the notes on the fridge, a gynecologist's card with an appointment marked in, Lukas's time-table, a flyer for a tango evening. Dance to silence, he read.

Have you started going to that again?

Astrid tipped coffee into the filter. I talked Rolf into giving it a try.

And will you let him lead you? asked Hubert.

If someone knows what he wants, I'll let myself be led, said Astrid.

She made the coffee, poured two cups, and gave one to him. He followed her into the living room where Lukas was playing with his Lego set. He wanted Hubert to play with him, but Astrid said there was something the grown-ups needed to discuss and went outside into the backyard. Hubert followed her across the little lawn and sat down under the sycamore on the rough bench he had built himself years ago. I'm amazed this is still in good shape, he said.

There are quite a lot of things of yours still here, said Astrid. That's what I wanted to talk to you about. I'd be glad if you would take them away with you.

What would I do with a bench? said Hubert. I don't have a garden.

I'm not talking about the bench, she said, I'm talking about your military uniform, your books, your records, your boyhood stuff, the telescope. The whole attic is full of your junk.

Hubert said he didn't have much space in his apartment and asked why the sudden hurry.

What do you mean, sudden hurry? she said. You moved out almost a year ago now. She took a sip of coffee and stood up. I asked Rolf if he wanted to move in, she said as she walked off.

Hubert caught up to her by the garage. She opened the door. His things were all piled up inside.

You can come for them when you're back.

Hubert drove home to finish packing for his trip. The whole time he was thinking about what he could possibly show. Late in the evening, he drove by the studio in the hope that his old stuff might inspire him, but it only depressed him. Astrid had asked him the other day for the photographs he had taken of her in the south of France. Hubert flicked through them and then put them up on a shelf with the other stuff. He had no intention of giving them to her.

He drove off in the morning. The sky was overcast, and it was raining lightly. Hubert left the Autobahn and took a gently climbing country road. The rain turned into snow, which fell more and more heavily in big, wet flakes. Hubert's first idea had been to take the mountain pass, but shortly before the turnoff he decided to put his car on the train. When he got to the ramp, a train had just left. He got out to stretch his legs. The air was freezing cold and smelled of snow and cow dung. He thought about how futile it would be to try and capture this scene in a painting, the late snow, the damp chilly air, the slopes that came in and out of view behind the veil of snowflakes, the crudity of the concrete ramp and the tunnel entrance.

In the tunnel, Hubert left the car lights off. It was shortly before noon, and he listened to the weather forecast on the radio. When the train emerged from the tunnel, there was snow only on the upper slopes. The valley was green.

Hubert could only vaguely remember the imposing two-story cultural center. It was set in a fairly narrow gorge that the River Inn had dug into the valley. Originally the building must have belonged to the old spa hotel next door. Outside the hotel, which was now run by a chain of vacation clubs, there was a large sign welcoming new guests: TIME FOR FEELING. As Hubert got out of the car, he saw through some trees a group of children in costume led by a woman also in costume, running shouting through the hotel grounds. On the well-kept lawn there were a few deck chairs, none of them occupied.

Hubert stepped into the arcade that led up to the entrance to the cultural center, but the front door was locked. There was no bell, and no one answered when he knocked. In the arcade were benches and a table tennis table, a couple of rusty bicycles were propped against the wall. Hubert walked around the building. Along the side, a few steps led down to a narrow path that followed an iron fence that continued along the back of the building. The other side of the fence was the riverbank. The Inn was a yellowish-gray, the current was rapid.

Grass and little bushes had taken root between the weathered concrete slabs of the path. Roughly in the middle of the wall was a door, presumably to the basement. On the ground in front of the gate and along the walls there were thousands of black ants.

When Hubert emerged back in front of the cultural center, there was another car parked next to his, a bottle-green Volvo, and the front door was open. He entered the hall, off which corridors opened to either side. Hubert followed one of them and on one of the last doors found a handwritten sign that said ADMINISTRATION.

No sooner had he knocked than the door flew open, and a stout man stood in front of him, who had to be around about the same age. He embraced Hubert and patted him on the shoulder. Hubert couldn't remember ever having seen him before.

They went out to the car park. Arno seemed astonished that Hubert had brought only a suitcase and a bag with him, and a couple of open cardboard boxes of slides and a projector.

No pictures, no materials? he asked.

Hubert said he hoped to generate the show here on the spot. Whatever materials he needed he would surely be able to obtain locally.

There's lots of leftover stuff from previous exhibitions up in the attic, said Arno, you can have a look around if you like. He picked up one of the boxes of slides and went

on ahead. For the moment you're our only resident artist,
he said, we were shut over the winter and only reopened a
few days ago. You can take your pick of the rooms.

After Arno had shown him all the rooms, Hubert chose
one that was large and almost empty, and a long way from
the office. Aside from the bed and a dark chest of drawers
there was a desk and a couple of old deep armchairs, but
neither a phone nor a TV. If Hubert wanted to call anyone, he could always do it from the office, said Arno, the
mobile connection was unfortunately very weak down in
the gorge. Hubert looked at his cell phone, which indeed
said NO RECEPTION. Arno said Hubert would have the building all to himself in the evenings. He brought the box of
slides in from the corridor where he had left it and set it
down in the middle of the room. Then he was suddenly
gone, and Hubert had to bring in the rest of his stuff by
himself. As there wasn't a wardrobe, he left his clothes in
the open suitcase and didn't unpack. He sat down on the
bed and stayed like that for a while. He remembered once
as a child having been sent up to a vacation camp in the
mountains. At midday the bus had stopped in front of a
large white house, and those children who had been there
before all rushed out into the dormitories to claim the
best places. By the time Hubert came up the steps, some
of them were already running the other way, to explore.
Hubert had sat all alone in the dormitory, not daring to go
out. For days he had been homesick and regretted that he
was not as enterprising and independent minded as the
others.

Hubert knocked on the office door. When he walked
in, the first thing to greet his eye was the poster of his

first exhibition hanging on the wall behind Arno, a rear view of a naked, rather lumpy woman washing her foot in a sink, presumably the best picture in the series. On the poster was the rather hopeless title of the show, *Begeg-nungen/Encounters*, with the dates, September 6–28, 2003.

I'm busy, said Arno, crumpling up a form and tossing it in the trash. Just have a look around and help yourself. If there's a problem, you know where to find me.

Hubert asked when the other artists would be arriving. Arno looked up from his work and shrugged. There's a young German woman who takes pictures of swimming pools. She's due soon, he said, but I don't know exactly when. Oh, yes, and someone from the local paper is coming to interview you. I hope four o'clock's okay with you?

Hubert walked through the building. Most of the other doors going off the corridor on either side were to rooms Arno had already showed him. One small room contained the toilets and three shower stalls. At the far end of the corridor was a kitchen with a long wooden table and an array of chairs of which no two were identical. The cupboards harbored pots and pans, dishes, and other gear. On one shelf were opened packets of dry goods, pasta, rice, lentils, chickpeas, and lots of jars and tins of all sorts of spices and condiments. Everything was coated with a sticky layer of grease, some of the dried herbs were years past their sell-by date.

That afternoon he sketched a rough layout of the entrance hall, which doubled as exhibition space, marking the position of outlets and measuring the height of the ceiling. He tried to remember his first exhibition here, but he had the impression he had never seen this room in his life. Finally he went for a walk to look at the locality. He crossed the old bridge beside the cultural center, which crossed the Inn. On the opposite side there was another, smaller building. Over the door he read SPA WATERS, and a scrap of paper taped to the glass door told him that the hall was closed, and no trespassing. Through the dirty windowpanes, Hubert saw evidence of former luxury, lofty pillars and three niches with polished stone facings, and the names of the respective sources over them: Lucius, Bonifacius, and Emerita.

The old road wound its way up the wooded slope. It was off-limits on account of building work, but there was no one to be seen, just a few machines had been left standing around. Hubert scrambled over the barrier and climbed on up the mountain. As he climbed, he kept checking his cell phone, but there was still no reception. He remembered that he hadn't eaten since breakfast, and he turned back. He decided to get something to eat in the hotel next door.

The sun outside was so dazzling that Hubert could see nothing at all when he walked into the lobby. The large room was full of old armchairs, in the middle was a bar, but there was no one around at all. At a desk behind reception, he finally saw a woman sitting at a computer. Hubert cleared his throat, and she got up. She walked up to the desk, parroting a greeting. She called Hubert "*du*" and explained that that was normal here, even before he could say what he had come for. The restaurant would open at six, she said, at the moment all the guests were out. But he could get coffee and cake here. Hubert thanked her and sat down in a leather armchair in a corner. After a while a young man dressed as a pirate came out and took his order. When the waiter brought his coffee, Hubert asked him about the costume and learned that there was a pirate-themed dinner tonight.

It's all in your weekly program, said the waiter.

I'm not staying at the hotel, said Hubert, and the waiter laughed as though he'd made a joke.

When Hubert returned to the cultural center a little before four, he saw a large heavyset man waiting in front of the building, with a camera and an enormous telephoto lens. He put out his hand and said he was from the local paper. He was a little early, but perhaps they could get the photos out of the way. While he took his pictures, he asked a few questions, from which Hubert guessed that the man had no idea who he was or what he was doing here. The answers seemed not to interest him either, presumably he just wanted Hubert's face to be in motion.

My colleague will be here in a minute to interview you, he said, after shooting off two dozen pictures.

Hubert sat down on one of the stone benches in the arcade, and the photographer sat opposite him. They sat there and waited in silence. After about a quarter of an hour, a tiny car drove up, and a black-haired young woman got out. Even as she approached the two men, she was apologizing for being late.

Tamara, she said and held out her hand to Hubert. Then she hugged the photographer. Hubert couldn't say if she'd kissed him on the mouth or not. The photographer went away. Tamara unpacked a small recording device and set it in front of her on the table. Then she winked at Hubert.

What may we expect from you? Are you still painting naked ladies?

Hubert hesitated.

Tamara said Arno had told her he wanted to develop his new show here in situ, but if he thought he would find models in the village he had another think coming. Because here everyone knew everyone else, and nobody was about to get her kit off for him. Suddenly her voice had an aggressive undertone. Hubert imagined her naked, with that expression on her face. He said he didn't yet know what the exhibition was going to contain. Tamara said he hadn't left himself very much time.

I know that, he said, irritated.

Then he remembered what she was there for and said he hoped to find inspiration here. The only driver for his work was desire, a kind of hunger for reality, for presence, and also for intimacy, as opposed to publicity. In a very wide sense, he was interested in transcendence.

Tamara looked as though she didn't believe a word of it. Do I have to warn the local women about you, or not? she asked.

He shook his head. I haven't painted any nudes for years.

She asked him a couple more standard questions about his life, his work at the college, and his plans for the future, then she got up, and so did Hubert.

Well, see you at the opening, if not before, she said, gave him her card, and got into her car.

The entrance to the cultural center was north facing and already in shade. The air was cold. Hubert went in to get a jacket and then he drove into the village and took a look around. The center of the village looked impressively unspoiled, there were many old buildings decorated with artful graffiti, some were festooned with Romansh proverbs, one had a sundial. The whole area must have been prosperous once, he thought, the boxy concrete hotels you found in other touristy places were completely absent.

After Hubert had wandered around for a while, he took a seat on a bench in a big square and watched the passersby. He thought about the exhibition. The village was lovely, the landscape was lovely, even the weather was lovely. He had grown up in a village himself, what was there to say about it? He should have known there was just as little for him here as there was at home.

The shadows had gotten longer, and when they stretched to cover the bench he was sitting on, Hubert felt the cold. He walked into the nearest restaurant, ordered a cup of tea, and checked his e-mails. Astrid had written, and so had Nina and a couple of the other students. The college invited him to a meeting and sent him the minutes for another. His gallerist asked him how he was getting on in the mountains and wrote to say he was looking forward to the opening. He asked Hubert to book him a room for the time.

Hubert answered evasively. By the time he was finished it was seven o'clock, and he ordered something to eat. The restaurant was almost empty, a few men were sitting at a round table drinking beer and arguing noisily about local politics. Shortly before nine, Hubert left the restaurant. He had drunk too much to drive, really.

The hotel was brightly lit. When Hubert parked his car, he heard voices and laughter from the grounds, and music. There were no lights on in the cultural center, the door was locked, and the building looked discouraging. Hubert groped for a light switch. In the kitchen he found half a bottle of grappa. He took it up to his room, set up the slide projector, and looked at the photographs of women he had taken back in the day. He didn't mean to work with the slides, presumably he had just brought them with him because they were part of the last sensible thing he had done. He projected the photos on a wall. He hadn't looked at them for years, in his memory they had been more interesting than they were. He was surprised at the impertinence with which he had proceeded, he must have been completely convinced by his work. Almost more surprising was that his self-assuredness and enthusiasm had been so contagious that he had found women who agreed to take part. In one of the photographs there was a small black-haired woman, a postwoman, whom he had run into at the end of her shift. She wedged a bottle of Prosecco between her thighs and fiddled with the cork. In the next picture she was reaching for glasses on a high shelf, in the third she was pouring wine into one of them and laughing because the bubbles overflowed the glass. Then there were two out-of-focus shots of her walking down the corridor, and one of her turning back the corner of her bed. That was the one and only time that Hubert had slept with one of his models. He had never used the photographs.

In the next slide tray there were photos of a woman of sixty or so, knitting, in a third a young woman breast-feeding her naked baby. She had struck an attitude and after the session asked him for copies of the pictures, which he had never sent her. These pictures had been useless as well. Hubert went through all his trays, pictures of more than forty women. Most of them he could just about remember, but in some of the latter trays he had the sense that he had never seen the pictures before. One sequence was taken in dim light, the pictures were slightly out of focus, and the face of the woman was never completely visible, sometimes she hid it behind her long hair, most of the time she was trying to avoid the camera anyway. Hubert couldn't quite remember her story, she was leaning across a table and seemed to be tidying up or looking at something. The room she was in seemed anonymous, other than the table there were no pieces of furniture or other objects to be seen. The pictures radiated a deep quiet, as though the model had been all alone in the room.

When he stood in the kitchen the next morning making coffee, Arno walked in. He said he had to go ahead and print up some exhibition posters, perhaps Hubert could let him have an image.

No, said Hubert.

A rough sketch? Anything at all? Is there a title for the show?

Hubert shook his head. Arno grimaced.

I suppose we can just print "Carte Blanche" on a white background, he said, what about that? Or better, white on black. Get it? He laughed. Have you seen the article?

He went off and reappeared a little later with a newspaper, which he laid on the table. Hubert took it back with him into his room. On the front page was a small photograph of him, with just his name, the word "painter," and the number of the page where the article could be found. There was another picture of him, and a reproduction of the poster for his previous exhibition. The article wasn't exactly hostile, but it had an ironic undertone. Tamara had gotten hold of biographical information (and misinformation) from Wikipedia. She referred briefly to the first exhibition in the cultural center, which had provoked a minor scandal, and wrote about Hubert's way of working. A few of the quotations must have been lifted from other interviews.

Hubert Amrhein's interest in naked ladies has worn off, wrote Tamara, he has matured, or perhaps simply got older, and he no longer scouts out naked bodies. There was a time when women had to go in fear of him, nowadays he is a spiritual seeker. It's not impossible that he will find what he is looking for here in our area.

Hubert had no idea what that was based on. He took the newspaper back to the office.

Arno looked up at him questioningly. Do you like the article?

The stuff about spirituality is nonsense, said Hubert, I have no idea what that's about.

Arno told him there were a lot of power places in the area, most artists who came here were interested in those.

Well, I'm not, said Hubert and he went back to his room.

That afternoon he went for a walk. He called Tamara and asked if she had time for coffee, he thought she had played pretty fast and loose with things he'd told her in her article.

Do you want right of reply?

Coffee would probably take care of it, he said, but I've got some things I want to ask you.

Okay, she said, come and meet me at my office at six.

Oh, the power places, snorted Tamara. That's a complicated story.

She jabbed at her salad, and Hubert wondered if that was everything, then she put down her fork and said she didn't believe in any of that stuff herself. But of course she couldn't print anything negative about it in the paper, there were lots of people who came here for precisely that.

There are a few standing stones and cup marks from the Bronze Age, sure enough, but the dowsers, the guys who run around here with pendulums, measuring Bovis units, and claiming the radio vitality here is as strong as Chartres Cathedral, I think they're bonkers.

She talked about an ethnologist who called himself a geobiologist and saw traces of a landscape deity called Ana everywhere around. The hills were her breasts, the valleys and sources her loins. Hubert recalled the landscapes of Georgia O'Keeffe, where the hills looked like the bodies of naked women.

Tamara called the waitress and asked for the bill. She said she was on her way to a meeting of the commune. Hubert insisted on paying. After she was gone, he stayed for a long time alone. He got a copy of the paper, reread the article about himself, and listened to the conversation of the men at the next table.

In the hotel, there again seemed to be plenty of activity when Hubert went over there for a nightcap. At the circular bar in the lobby there were only couples and a group of young men, talking and laughing loudly. Opposite Hubert stood a woman between two men, who were talking over her head. She had blond hair and very pale skin, in the dark room it looked like she had been picked out by a spotlight. She seemed unconcerned, as though she had fallen into a kind of rigidity. Even when his eyes briefly met hers, Hubert saw no reaction in them. He drew her face on the back of a coaster. That made him think of a series of tourist portraits on coasters, but he was sure he would reject the idea when he was sober.

The next morning Hubert breakfasted in the hotel. It was already quite late, the few guests were mostly young couples. Hubert wondered what they were doing here and imagined spending a few days here with Nina. When the staff began clearing away the buffet, he went to reception, asked what a room cost, and also if he could pay to use the pool. You mean the spa and recreation area, said the receptionist, and quoted a rather steep price. Hubert thanked her and strolled through the hotel. The building looked a little faded and dim, although lights were on all over the place. From a second-story window he surveyed the grounds, where a few children sat in a circle with a young woman, tossing a ball around. A few elderly visitors read or snoozed in deck chairs, even though it was ten in the morning.

Hubert went back downstairs and scanned the hotel notice board, the week's program, the day's menu, looked at a poster of protected Alpine flowers that was familiar to him from boyhood, and studied what to do in the event of a forest fire. Then there was an organizational chart of the hotel, with the first names and functions of every employee. Over each name was a small photograph, almost all of them showed smiling young people in red polo shirts, most of the women had long hair, many of them were blond. One face was familiar to Hubert: JILL, HEAD OF ENTERTAINMENT, it said under the picture. Gillian's face looked a little different from before, but that might just be the photo. He looked around, as though he'd been doing something forbidden, and quickly left the hotel.

He walked down a narrow footpath along the river and thought of his last meeting with Gillian, and how he had thrown her out of his studio.

At the end of his walk, he went briefly into the cultural center to fetch his swimming trunks. He had no plan to get in touch with Gillian, but he was drawn back to the hotel. In the pool there were a few people copying exercises demonstrated by a young man on the poolside. Hubert went into the sauna, but the heat was soon too much for him. When he returned to the pool, it was full of shouting children. He watched them for a while, then went to the changing room. All the time he was thinking of Gillian, and preparing an account for what had happened then. As he walked past reception, he stopped on impulse and asked about her. The woman at the desk asked him for his name and made a quick phone call.

She's just on her way, she said.

Hubert sat down in his old leather armchair in the lobby.

Five minutes later, Gillian was standing in front of him. He pushed himself up with both hands, and for a moment they stood uncertainly facing each other. Gillian's face looked somehow incoherent, she had slight scarring, like someone with bad acne in childhood, and her nose looked different, it seemed cruder, a little puffy.

She smiled, kissed Hubert on the cheek, and asked him if he wanted to have a drink.

Do you have time? he asked.

She nodded and said the preseason was pretty quiet. Come on, let's go outside.

She led him across the hall. She was wearing a red polo shirt with the hotel logo on it, and tight white pants.

The terrace was at the back of the hotel and gave onto the grounds. Only one of the tables was occupied, by two old couples sitting together over beer and cards. Gillian sat down and waved to the waiter. She ordered a white wine spritzer. Hubert followed suit. While waiting for their drinks, neither of them spoke.

Gillian raised her glass, smiled, and said I go by Jill here, it's easier for people to say.

Again, neither of them spoke.

It seems to me I have every reason to be angry, she then said, smiling again.

Hubert nodded and was a little surprised at his willingness to accept the blame.

How did you find me? Did Arno say something?

Hubert said it had been pure chance, he had seen her picture on the hotel notice board. I'm doing another exhibition at the cultural center.

I know, said Jill. I saw the article in the paper, though it didn't tell me much.

Me either, said Hubert. It's all so long ago, I can hardly remember.

I suppose it was my idea to have you back, said Jill. I'm on the committee that runs the cultural center. My last connection to the arts.

Why didn't you get in touch? he asked.

Jill made a face. You made it pretty clear last time that you weren't interested in me.

My wife left me, said Hubert.

Jill didn't respond and asked instead what he was planning to show. Hubert shrugged. He laughed uncertainly. Suddenly Jill stood up, finished her spritzer, and said she had to go back to work.

Come and have dinner sometime. Are you free on Sunday?

I'm always free, he said.

Then come and meet me here at six.

She bent down, kissed him on the cheek, and disappeared.

There was a knock on the door, Hubert was still in bed. It's me, said Arno, can we talk?

I'll come down, said Hubert.

He waited for the footfall of the director to disappear, then he went to the bathroom. Twenty minutes later, he was standing in front of Arno's desk like a naughty pupil told to see the principal. Do you need anything? asked Arno. Is there some way I can help...

Hubert lied that he had an idea but wasn't able to say anything specific about it.

We're under a certain amount of pressure here, said Arno, some local politicians resent us, and we need proof that we're doing good work. It's important that the show be a success.

I'll keep you posted, said Hubert

Just do something, said Arno. Anything, so long as we don't have bare walls in three weeks.

Hubert breakfasted in the hotel. Then he got the password for the WLAN and Googled Gillian's name. A couple hundred mentions came up, but almost all of them seemed to be about her former work in TV. When he put Jill for Gillian, there were fewer than a dozen results, and they all had to do with her work in the vacation club.

The opening of the graduation show at the art college was scheduled for Friday. Hubert had promised Nina and the others he would be there, but he was just on his way out of the cultural center when he saw on the door a large black poster with *Carta Alba/Carte Blanche* on it, his name, and the dates of the show. The opening was in exactly three weeks, on June 25. He decided not to drive down into the valley and instead went to the hotel and sat in the lobby. He wrote Nina an apologetic e-mail. He was under pressure, didn't know what to do, couldn't get away. He promised to come down in the next week or two to take a look at her work.

When he drove down to the village later on to buy food, he saw the poster for his exhibition in some of the shop windows. It felt as though Arno was making fun of him.

He spent the evening in the hotel lobby, aimlessly surfing the Web.

On Saturday morning, Hubert called Astrid. She asked how he was doing and whether the show was coming together. He replied evasively. They talked about a few practical matters, then Astrid asked if she and Lukas should come up and see him. Maybe Rolf would come too. Hubert said it wasn't a good time, he needed to concentrate on what he was doing. Then he asked to talk to Lukas and asked him what he was doing, but the boy was pretty monosyllabic and soon hung up.

All Sunday Hubert was nervous. He had crazy ideas about what he might do for the show, he thought about unpacking his old slides, projecting them on the walls or magnifying them, the whole series as a sort of illustrated romance. He could cut bits out of them, blow up certain details till they became unrecognizable. Or take pictures of himself, naked or clothed, doing the same things he had painted the women doing, as an ironic commentary on his earlier exhibition. Or he could do the thing he thought about doing before, make portraits of hotel guests. Or he could start a herbarium, paint with natural materials, make a stone circle, some reference to the power places. He even briefly considered a performance, though that really wasn't his thing. None of it interested him.

In the afternoon, he took himself to the hotel spa. At six he asked at reception for Jill. He was told she would be on her way, but it was another ten minutes before she appeared in the lobby.

We can take my car, she said, leaving the hotel almost at a run.

She had a red Twingo, the backseat was a jumble of papers and clothes. Jill drove fast up the narrow road and over the new bridge.

Don't you live in the village, then? asked Hubert.

Just outside, said Jill, it's not far.

Five minutes later, she drew up outside a 1950s vacation house.

It's not a thing of beauty, she said, but it belongs to my parents, so there's no rent to pay.

How long have you been living here? asked Hubert.

Six years. I moved up here right after the accident.

Hubert said he had read something about that in a magazine, what had happened.

Jill climbed out. While they were still standing in front of the house, she explained rapidly that her husband had been drunk, had hit a deer, and died.

I was pretty badly hurt. My nose was more or less gone, but they built me another one that's almost the same. It took over three years and lots of operations before it looked all right. Come in. Do you want a tour?

She showed him around and talked about the oil-fired central heating that would have to be replaced sometime, and the fact that they could do a roof conversion if they ever needed more space. The décor looked impersonal, perhaps because a lot of the furniture was old and didn't really belong, as though its useful life had been spent somewhere else, and it was here in semiretirement. On the walls were a couple of calendar photos of Engadin landscapes, which Jill certainly wouldn't have chosen. The magnificent landscape outside reappeared inside, in smaller, faded versions. On the dining table was a thick mustard yellow cloth, with

a wrought iron ashtray on it. The air smelled of cold cigarette smoke.

They sat at a little granite table in the garden, in the
middle of a flower meadow ringed by tall shrubbery. The
sun hadn't gone yet, but the light was changing, and large
flecks of shade were wandering over the facing slopes.

I get properly snowed in here sometimes, said Jill. I've
more or less got used to the mountains, but the winters are
very long here.

How on earth did you wind up doing this vacation club
thing? asked Hubert.

I had to do something, said Jill. I couldn't go back in
front of the camera, and I didn't want to retreat into editorial. I came here because I wanted to recuperate for a
while, then I saw a job ad and applied. At first I was working with children. The good thing is that ninety-nine per-
cent of our guests are from Germany. No one recognized
me. My boss was the only one who knew I'd once worked in
TV. I told everyone who wanted to hear about it about the
accident, and after that people no longer asked. Anyway,
my nose kept looking better after each operation. Once I
had settled, there was an opening in events, and my boss
offered me the job.

And what do you do there? asked Hubert.

We put on an event every other evening, plays, musi-
cals, sing-alongs. I'm also responsible for sports and fitness, I draw up schedules, look after my team. And I'm
very often out with guests, we go on hikes together, I play
games with them, sometimes do a little bit of acting. I just
about have enough talent for the kind of things we put on.
Tomorrow we're doing *Love Between Valley and Peak*, you can

come if you like, I'll save you a seat. I'm playing the farm
er's ugly daughter.

Hubert stared at Jill. She looked back, unabashed.

The play wasn't as silly as it sounded, she said, at any
rate it was perfect for the guests. And she got a kick out of
being onstage again. It was only here that I realized how
heartily sick I was of the arts scene in the city.

She asked Hubert what he had done in all that time.
He talked about his teaching job and the fact that he had
almost stopped painting. I don't know why that is, he said.
Maybe I've just seen too much bad art, my own included.

By now the sun had disappeared behind the mountains, and the shadows were creeping up the slopes.

I'm cold, said Jill, shall we go inside?

Hubert followed her into the house and then into the
kitchen. She opened the fridge and looked uncertainly at
what little it contained. I'm afraid I haven't bought anything wonderful, she said. What do you feel like eating?

Perhaps I just need to reconcile myself to the fact that
people want pictures to hang on their walls, said Hubert,
and watched as Jill washed lettuce and cut a carrot in sliv-
ers. It's not a crime. But I think I'd rather work on a building site or wait tables than make commercial art.

Stay here, said Jill, I can make inquiries at the hotel.
You could offer drawing classes to the guests, I'm sure that
would go down well. She was facing away from him, and
for a moment he thought she meant it. She turned and
passed him the salad bowl with a grin.

During the meal, Jill talked about the club, and meetings with hotel guests, personnel difficulties, and the one
big family they were.

When I began here, I looked so horrible, I'm surprised they gave me a job at all. Hang on.

She brought out another bottle of wine and went over to a small desk by the window, opened a drawer, and pulled out a cardboard folder that she laid in front of Hubert. She sat down beside him and opened the folder. He saw a photograph in which she looked more or less as he saw her now. She went on, and from page to page her face changed. It looked as though it was crumbling, even though it was always the same face. Sometimes Hubert clutched Jill's hand and asked her to go back one. Then there was a picture of Jill's nose, which looked like a large red potato, and another in which her whole face was cut and bloody. It was so swollen around the eyes that he could hardly see them, and everywhere there were patches of raw flesh. There was no nose.

That's what I looked like after the accident, said Jill. They took the photos in the hospital.

Hubert turned away. It wasn't the last picture, but Jill dwelled on it for a long time before turning the page. The next was a portrait of her as she was at the time Hubert had met her. Her face had an expression of vulnerability, as though she sensed what was in store for it. But it was only when he saw the next picture that he realized where these pictures came from. Jill was sitting naked on a chair in his studio, her hands in her lap, a pose he had cribbed from Edvard Munch. These were the pictures he had taken then. They were better than he had thought at the time. He remembered accusing Jill of not being there and of being stilted. He picked up the rest of the pictures, laid them on the table side by side, and stood up so he was able to see them all together. A few were shots of her upper body, or her face.

Do you like them? she asked.

Hubert suddenly remembered her provocative question to him when she had taken her clothes off. Do you like what you see, then?

Yes, he said. Presumably something could have been done with these.

He also spread out the photos of Jill's injured face.

They have more to do with one another than you might think, she said. If my husband hadn't seen these shots of yours, the accident wouldn't have happened.

She refilled their glasses and lit a cigarette. That's a frightening thought, isn't it, that you're capable of killing someone with your art.

He put the photographs on the table into two piles: the nude shots and the injured faces.

Do you want me to exhibit these?

I don't know, said Jill. You're the artist.

She had been smoking one cigarette after the other, now clouds of smoke hung under the low ceiling. Hubert wanted to open a window, but when he stood up he almost overbalanced and had to grab hold of Jill's chair. She stood up as well, and the chair fell over. They held each other.

Come, she said. He looked in her eyes, but their look was expressionless. It was chilly in the bedroom and smelled of wood and old smoke.

When Hubert awoke, he felt giddy, but at least he didn't have a headache. He was dressed. Next to him lay Jill, apparently asleep. She was wearing a short silk night-dress, which had ridden up a little. He stroked her, felt her coming around, though she didn't move. After a time she turned and looked at Hubert.

What time is it?

Without answering, he laid his hand on her stomach and went on stroking her. Jill smiled. When he slipped his hand down between her legs, she gripped it tight.

Draw me.

Hubert groaned.

There's a pad and pencils on my desk downstairs, she said.

He groaned again, got up, and went downstairs. When he came back, she was undressed. She was lying on her stomach, her head pillowed on her crossed arms.

Hubert sat on a chair and drew her. As soon as he stopped, Jill changed position, and he turned the page and started a new sketch. She lay on her side; with her upper body raised; kneeling, hands behind her back; standing with folded arms by the window; sitting on a chair, legs apart, hands on her knees.

After he had done about twenty drawings, Jill went up to him and propped her hands on her hips. Let's see what you've done.

Hold that, he said and sat on the bed to go on drawing.

Turn around.

He made a couple more drawings until Jill said she was hungry and had to have a cup of coffee and a cigarette. They ate breakfast in the sunshine outside.

Well, that seemed to work all right, said Jill.

Hubert shook his head. Those were just finger exercises.

Jill leafed through the pad on the table in front of them.

I like your drawings.

Of course I can knock out a couple of nudes, said Hubert, but that doesn't prove anything.

I think I expected to be told something about myself from your pictures, said Jill, but then I saw you didn't see me at all. That's what made me undress. The notion that a human being should be something sealed off like a table or a chair is nonsense. Eventually I was reconciled to the thought that I didn't really exist.

She went on leafing through the drawings.

The thing about the drawing lessons here, by the way, I meant that. They don't need to be life classes. If you're going to be spending more time here. You'd be paid for it, maybe it would inspire you.

Hubert was pushing buttons on his phone. There's no reception here either, he said.

He spent the next several days driving around the area, even though he felt tired and unwell. He took photographs of the landscape that he knew he would never use. It was pleasant and warm. Sometimes he parked his car and walked some way up a slope, but he never went very far. When he ran into Arno, Arno always looked at him reproachfully. Once, Hubert asked him when the other artists were arriving. Arno shrugged and said they were delayed, he had no exact information.

On Thursday Hubert took the train down into the valley and spent the weekend in the city without getting in touch with Nina or Astrid, or taking in the diploma exhibition. Arno tried to speak with him once or twice, but each time Hubert refused the call. Instead, he called Jill and made a date for Saturday.

This time they went to a restaurant in the village. In the car, Jill asked Hubert where he had been, Arno had been desperately looking for him. We have the events committee tomorrow afternoon. He's afraid you won't be ready in time. It's in less than two weeks. He's thinking of trying to bring in someone else instead at short notice. Hubert didn't say anything.

After dinner, Jill quite naturally drove back to her house. They split a bottle of wine and talked about the past six years. At midnight Jill asked if Hubert wanted to stay the night. Again, they slept in the same bed.

When Hubert awoke, Jill was already up, and he could smell coffee. Over breakfast she said she had to get going, but he didn't have to hurry. Just call Arno.

Hubert didn't feel like going to the cultural center and getting leaned on, so instead he showered and then wandered farther on up the road out of the village. It climbed a little more, and wound among meadows with large rocks lying on them, and then it went down, and he arrived in a thin forest. The air was cool and damp and resinous and ever so slightly smoky. Sunbeams fell through the trees and cast blurred patterns on the forest floor. He sat on a thick tree trunk by the side of the road and listened to the birds. He could hear the rushing of the Inn down below. He remembered walks he had gone on with his parents, vacation weeks in the mountains, endless days spent building dams over mountain streams, playing hide-and-seek in the forest, making campfires and cooking sausages. Suddenly he heard a buzzing sound. He looked down at his cell and

saw he had five text messages. Three were from Arno, who
wrote that there was an important meeting today, and
would Hubert get in touch, urgently. The fourth was from
Astrid, who asked how he was doing. She was planning on
coming to the opening. Nina had written some nonsense.
Hubert wiped everything and put the phone back in his
pocket.

He walked back to Jill's house, did the dishes, and
picked a bunch of wildflowers from the garden. He
couldn't find a vase, so he used a big beer glass. Then he
looked around the house once more. The books on Jill's
shelves were surely mostly her parents'. Everywhere in
the house lay piles of magazines and fashion papers, in
the living room next to the sofa was a stereo, beside it a
little shelf with a couple dozen CDs. Hubert sat down at
Jill's desk and opened a drawer. He leafed through her old
calendars, which he found right at the back. Most of the
entries seemed to be about her work, plus a few massage
or pedicure appointments, and sometimes a name without time or comment. Mostly they were women's names,
and they came around fairly regularly.

It was just two o'clock. Hubert went back out into the
garden. He took a piece of wood from the pile next to the
door, sat down at the granite table, and started whittling
away at it with his pocket knife. He didn't carve a shape,
but first took off the bark, then cut the wood patiently
into thin strips. As a boy he had often whiled away the
hours like this, had pulled one thread after another from
a piece of rough cloth, or picked away at a rope until
there were just thin fibers left, broken up a blossom or

a fir twig into its constituent parts, hatched and cross-hatched a piece of paper with pencil till it made a shiny even surface. Suddenly he saw the exhibition he wanted to put on: white steles distributed around a room, and on them the remnants of such labors, a pile of thread, hemp fibers, blossoms. Or, better, he would leave the steles empty, and the materials would lie beside them on the floor, as though rejected, or as though the objects had dissolved of their own accord. He went into the house, got a small plastic bag from the kitchen, and put in the wood shavings and the rest of the log.

He made his way back to the cultural center. He was pretty sure that Arno would be underwhelmed by his idea, but he didn't care. It had sprung organically from the situation in which he found himself and was the logical continuation of his earlier work. Whereas he had always been at pains to arrest time, now for the first time it would be incorporated into his work. He doubted that anyone would notice, but the main thing was that it convinced him.

In the cultural center, he headed straight to Arno to tell him the good news, but he wasn't in his office. Presumably the committee meeting was in progress where they were talking about the exhibition. He thought of calling him, but he liked the idea of the committee racking their brains over something while he had already solved their problem for them. He would tell Jill about his project tonight, that was plenty early enough.

He drove down into the village to buy the things he needed, a rope, soft pencils, a few coarsely woven red place mats that would be easy to pull apart. Then he drove back to the cultural center and climbed up to the attic. The roof wasn't insulated and it was warm in the long space, and smelled of dust and old junk. There were all kinds of things standing around, and after looking for a while, Hubert found a dozen white steles. They were a little tall to be ideal. He carted six of them down to the ground floor and carried them into the kitchen and washed them with warm water and soap. They were full of spiderwebs, and it took a long time to get them more or less clean. Then he stood them up in the entrance hall and tried out what their best positions were. In the end, he decided to stand them all in a row.

Jill was waiting in the hotel lobby.

No sooner had they sat down than Jill said she had some good news for Hubert. And I've got some for you, he said. You start.

We've found someone to stand in for you, said Jill, a young woman artist from Germany who was going to come up anyway. Thea Genser, perhaps you know her? Arno talked to her on the phone a couple of days ago, now she's coming a little earlier than planned and bringing a series with her that she's completed recently.

Hubert shook his head and smiled, that wouldn't be necessary, he had had an idea himself.

When? asked Jill.

Hubert told her of his plan.

But we've committed to Thea now, said Jill. She's been here before too.

You could at least have spoken to me, said Hubert.

Arno was trying to reach you all this time, said Jill, but you kept ignoring him. I'll try and have a word with him.

The dining room was starting to empty when a young man joined them. When he had finished his plate of hors d'oeuvres and went up to the buffet, Jill explained that it was part of the concept of the vacation club that no one was to sit alone. Hubert wouldn't have minded talking to her quietly a little longer, but now the young man cut in and told them about a hike he'd been on. Twelve hundred meters, up and down, he said. Jill praised his fitness. When she got up to get her dessert, she laid her hand briefly on his shoulder. Hubert followed her to the buffet, but only to get a cup of coffee.

Who the hell is that? he asked. Is there something going on between the two of you?

It's part of the job, explained Jill. It's called talking to the guests.

What if the guest gets on your wick? asked Hubert.

No sooner had Jill finished her apple strudel than she said she had to get changed and made up for her performance.

Will we meet at the bar later?

After she was gone, the young man told Hubert the whole story of his hike again, as though he hadn't heard it already. Hubert got up and went over to the bar.

There were a few couples on sofas and armchairs by the windows, in their midst stood a hotel employee asking questions in a broad Frankish accent. It seemed to be a kind of quiz, whoever knew the answer had to call out a word, Hubert didn't understand it.

He went outside for a stroll in the grounds. When he

came back, the doors to the theater were open, he sat as far away from the two dozen or so hotel guests who were waiting for the show to begin. The young man from dinner was sitting in the front row.

The play was banal enough, but for all that Hubert sometimes had to laugh. The other members of the audience seemed to entertain no reservations. In one scene the beautiful daughter emptied a full chamber pot over the ugly sister's dress. Jill had to take off her dirndl and stand there onstage in old-fashioned underwear, which brought her a separate little round of applause. She wasn't especially good, though better than the others, and she clearly enjoyed it. At the end, even the ugly daughter got her man, Toni, a yokel in lederhosen. To tumultuous applause the cast bowed, and the lights came on.

Hubert waited at the bar, but instead of Jill there was Arno suddenly in front of him. He was carrying a roll of paper under his arm. Jill called me, he said.

I've got an idea for the exhibition, said Hubert.

I'm sorry, but it's too late, said Arno. Hubert thought he could detect some schadenfreude in his voice. I've covered over all the posters. He unrolled one of the pale blue posters he was carrying. Thea Genser, *Durch Wasser/Through Water*.

She takes pictures of empty swimming pools in winter, said Arno, it's outstanding work.

I don't understand the title, said Hubert. He ordered another beer and watched Jill and the young man from dinner in animated conversation. Arno said he had to go on. Hubert took his glass and went over to Jill, who was just laughing heartily.

Armin was suggesting I always wore underwear like that.

He can't actually be that stupid, said Hubert.

They were both silent.

I think he wants to get inside your pants himself, said Hubert.

Excuse me, said Jill to Armin.

She took Hubert by the arm and walked him over to the door.

Will you please stop insulting our guests, she said. I think it's best you go home.

I'm not at home here, he said and emptied his glass.

Jill took it from him and said, if he liked, he could spend the night at her house.

When Hubert woke up, Jill was standing by the window, opening the curtains. The sun was shining. Jill went to him and sat on the edge of the bed.

Sleep well?

What time did you get home? he asked.

Not so late that I had trouble getting up in the morning. If you want to have breakfast with me, you'd better get a move on.

After Jill had gone off to work, Hubert looked up his e-mails on her computer and answered the most urgent ones. Although he had been pretty drunk the night before, he had taken the car. Now he walked to the cultural center, he was in no particular hurry.

In front of the building was an old minivan with German plates. A young woman was carrying a big wooden crate inside. Hubert held the door open for her. Only then did he notice the light blue poster that had been plastered over the larger, black one, giving the appearance of a window in a dark room. The steles he had set up yesterday in the entrance hall were parked in a corner, on the floor was a pile of aluminum frames in bubble wrap. The young woman had been in one of the guest rooms, and shortly after she came back. She walked up to Hubert and held out her hand. Hi, I'm Thea. Hubert, he said. Oh, she said. Well, I hope you don't mind that I'm having the exhibition here now. He shrugged and grabbed one of the steles and carried it up to his room.

He spent the rest of the day pulling single threads out of the place mats, until there were just enough left for one to guess the original shape and size. Music started playing in the building, punctuated by the unctuous voice of a radio announcer. Hubert went into the entrance hall, where Thea was just unpacking her pictures and propping them against the wall. On the floor among the packing materials was a tinny little transistor radio. He asked her if she'd mind switching it off.

No problem, she said.

I can't work with that sort of noise going on, Hubert said tetchily.

No problem, repeated Thea. I had no idea you were still around.

In the evening, Hubert went for a walk. He followed the road to Jill's house. Behind him he heard a car. Only when it pulled up alongside him did he realize it was Jill.

She wound down the window and asked if he was going somewhere.

It was cold in the house. Jill hadn't turned on any lights. The blue sky through the windows reminded Hubert of the poster for Thea's show. Jill sat down with him and lit a cigarette.

What sort of farce was that?

You mean the play yesterday? asked Jill. That's just for fun, you mustn't take it seriously.

I mean the whole thing, said Hubert. The invitation to the cultural center, and then your taking the exhibition away from me in the eleventh hour, in favor of a girl who's barely got her diploma. And you in this ridiculous hotel, you can't mean it. That's not you.

Maybe not, said Jill, but life here is less of a strain. Our guests like to have a bit of fun, that's what they're paying for, and when they get it, they're grateful and satisfied.

They sat facing each other in silence.

To begin with, I took an ironic view of everything here, said Jill finally, but over time I got to be really fond of the people. You'd be surprised at who comes here for vacations.

Hubert made to speak, but Jill cut him off.

I think I wanted to show you that. Because of the way you cut me down to size and said I wasn't there. She stood up and made an actorish bow to him, and smiled. Well? Do you like what you see?

The last remaining days before the opening Hubert worked incessantly. He had set out the steles in his room. On one he put the rest of the log he had whittled, and at its foot the whittlings, on the next the frayed place mats, and on the ground the red threads he had pulled out. Over one stele he looped the picked-at rope. He started covering some pieces of paper with pencil hatchings till gleaming black surfaces resulted, where the individual lines were no longer visible. Sometimes the paper was rubbed through or got warped in the course of the work, but he didn't mind.

Thea spent days over the hanging of her pictures. Each time Hubert left his room, he found her standing in the exhibition space with a framed picture in her hand or on the floor at her feet. In the evening, Hubert left the cultural center and drove into the village to eat in a restaurant there. Then he would look up his e-mails. Astrid wrote that she was coming to the opening with Lukas and Rolf, perhaps he could reserve them a room in a nice hotel. Nina similarly said she would be coming for the opening, and bringing a couple of friends. He deleted the e-mails without answering them, he had to concentrate on his work.

He only went into the kitchen in the morning, to fix coffee. He no longer appeared at the hotel. What little he needed he bought in the village store. Some days he ate nothing but salted peanuts, until his mouth was burning with them, and drank copious amounts of coffee. He slept badly and had wild dreams from which he often woke bathed in sweat. Sometimes he had the feeling that everything he perceived stood in some relation to his slow work of destruction, the way the light crept over the floor, the rushing of the river audible inside, the cries of the children in the hotel grounds. He tore a piece out of an old shirt and then used a needle to pick thread after thread out of it. The weave was so fine that he needed the lens of his slide projector as a magnifying glass. After he had spent hours working, he pushed everything aside, only to begin right away on the next task. For many hours on end he was unaware of time passing.

The final will is that to be truly present.
So that the lived moment belongs to us and we to it...

ERNST BLOCH

Jill had gone over to the window of her office and was looking out onto the grounds behind the hotel. It was a gorgeous day, almost all the deck chairs were occupied, children were playing in the meadow, and in the background, in the shade of some mighty trees that stood by the riverbank, a dozen guests were sitting in a circle. Most were barefoot, some only in shorts and T-shirt. They had sketch pads on their knees and were attentively watching Hubert, who was standing in their midst, talking. On a basket chair next to him sat a naked young woman. Hubert gestured expansively, it was as though he was painting a picture in the air.

His course was a rip-roaring success. Jill could have filled it twice over, that's how many people had signed up for it. A model was easily found as well: Ursina, the masseuse who had a practice in the village and came to the hotel when required. Jill knew that Ursina had sometimes done modeling when she was a student, and she agreed without demur. She seemed completely uninhibited, stretching during breaks or walking around to inspect the guests' handiwork. Jill waved at Hubert, but he didn't see her, and she sat down at her desk to finish the schedules for the next month.

Hubert had recovered remarkably quickly from his breakdown. On the morning of the opening, Jill had been seriously worried about him. Arno had called her and told her to come right away. It was her day off, and she was still in her nightie, but fifteen minutes later she was standing next to Arno in Hubert's room in the cultural center. Hubert was deathly pale, he had beads of sweat on his brow. Jill called the doctor, then she got a large glass of water from the kitchen. You're dehydrated, she said to Hubert, and helped him to sit up. The doctor prescribed something to lower his blood pressure, but what he needed above all was rest.

My wife is coming, and so are three of my students, said Hubert. They're under the impression that I've got a show.

Is that all you're worried about? said Jill. Come on, I'll take you back to my place, no one will think of looking for you there.

During the first few days at Jill's, Hubert wasn't up to much. When she asked him in the evening what he had done during the day, he shrugged. After a few days he began to read. Most of the books in the house were Jill's mother's, they were illustrated guides to the area, cookbooks, and English novels. This rather random library had led to an improvement of relations between Jill and her mother. There was nothing arcane about her mother's handwritten marginalia in the cookbooks, but they showed Jill a life that had had no other end in view than to provide a good home for her husband and daughter.

Ever since Jill had moved into the vacation home, her parents came up less frequently. Jill's father had bad knees, and the stairs were difficult for him. If they went anywhere for vacation, it was to spa hotels, where he could receive physiotherapy.

Hubert seemed to read anything that fell into his hands, a collection of local legends, a book of Alpine flora, a little volume of Engadin proverbs that were painted all over the houses hereabouts.

It's easy to find fault, and harder to do, he read. There must have been an artist living in that house. Or what about this: A little wolf is present in every one of us.

Jill was in the kitchen, making their dinner.

Love your destiny, even if it is bitter, read Hubert. Do you think that's true?

Why don't you wash the lettuce, said Jill.

When she came home the next day, Hubert was sitting in front of the house, sketching. She walked around and looked over his shoulder. He was just copying a sgraffito from the book of proverbs. He leafed back through the pad and showed her the drawings he had done, careful copies of mermaids, crocodiles, and zodiacs graced with sayings. He tore out a sheet and handed it to her. A year is long, ten years are short, she read.

They shared a bed. Jill went to the bathroom first. When Hubert had turned out the light and lain down next to her, she sometimes scooted over to him, and they would embrace. When Jill turned around, she felt Hubert's erection. Neither of them said anything, and after a while, Jill crept back to her side of the bed. One evening she asked him in earnest whether he would like to conduct a drawing class in the club and was astonished when he immediately said yes.

Jill was happier than she'd been for a very long time. Only now did she realize how solitary she had been these past years. When she remembered the time with Matthias, it was as though it had nothing to do with her present life. The memory of the sessions with Hubert, on the other hand, had remained vivid.

After she had talked Arno into inviting Hubert to hold another exhibition in the cultural center, she had been anxious for weeks. Then, when he sat in front of her in the hotel lobby again, everything was the way it had been before. And since Hubert had started living with her, she looked forward to coming home every evening. He frequently did the cooking. After dinner they often sat outside the house for hours, talking.

The first course Hubert offered was in landscape painting. A half dozen guests signed up for it. In the evening Jill met one of the participants, an old lady who had come with her granddaughter and had taken the course with her. The woman was enthusiastic, even her granddaughter had enjoyed it. Hubert too appeared to have enjoyed the day. When Jill came home, he had dinner ready. Well, how was it? she asked.

It's amazing how many people paint in their free time, he said. There are no great geniuses among them, but at least they're not beginners either.

You seem to have an admirer, said Jill.

Hubert looked at her with round eyes, then he said: Oh, do you mean Elena? She's a teenager.

Actually, I was thinking of her grandmother, said Jill, laughing.

Since there were guests who stayed at the club for two weeks and wanted to carry on painting, Hubert offered a further course the following week, in portraiture. Obviously word had got out that he was a good teacher, at any rate the enrollment was twice the first week's. At the end of the week, Jill asked him whether he would like to teach life drawing as well, that would certainly interest the younger set. And will you sit for us? he asked. If I can't find anyone else I will, said Jill.

Most of the participants in the life-drawing class were men. Sometimes in the evening Hubert showed Jill sketches he had made of the students: malicious little caricatures of a shy young fellow who hardly dared look up from his page; a fat, bald fifty-year-old who as he worked jammed the tip of his tongue between his lips; another, still older man whose eyes were wide with terror as though they had seen Death. We'll hang them up in the lobby next week, said Jill, to help recruit the next group.

Hubert spent more and more time at the club. Jill saw him from her window talking to the guests or disappearing with a group of youths in the direction of the football field. In the evening he would collect her in her office.

Do you want to take the car? she asked. I'm acting tonight.

It was the same play Hubert had seen her in before. He said he would stay and watch it again, maybe he would find some hidden depths in it this time. They ate together on the terrace, then he walked her to the tiny dressing room behind the stage. The costumes hung in the props room, a windowless annex stuffed full of scenery, clothes stands, and props that were used in the various productions. The dressing room was jammed full, but no one seemed to object to Hubert's presence there. Jill loved the atmosphere of the performances, her male and female colleagues were excited, saying break a leg and pretending to spit over one another's shoulders.

Hubert stood in the wings for the whole performance, watching. When Jill had an exit, she remained standing so close to him that he could feel the warmth of her body. He whispered something, but she covered his mouth with her hand. The audience laughed, and Jill had to go out again, to receive the contents of the chamber pot over her dress. For the final ovation the cast dragged Hubert out onto the stage with them, even though he had contributed nothing to the performance, and he laughed and bowed along with the others.

Most of them had kept their costumes on and headed straight for the bar to celebrate with the guests, and Jill and Hubert were the last two in the dressing room. Jill had hung up the wet dirndl to dry. In her old-fashioned undies she sat in front of one of the two mirrors, her face shining. Hubert had disappeared into the props room, and Jill was taking off her makeup. Suddenly he stood behind her, in lederhosen and checkered shirt, almost the identical costume to the yokel whom Jill had married in the play.

Aren't you natty, she said, laughing and getting up. You should wear lederhosen more often.

Hubert took a step toward her and took her in his arms and kissed her on the mouth.

Toni! How could you! she resumed her role. You could at least wash your hands after milking.

Toni's answer was a certain laugh line in every performance, but Hubert didn't speak, just went on kissing Jill. He held her so hard it almost hurt. She responded to his kiss, and as though that was an invitation, he started undressing her. He kissed her on the throat and collarbone, and when they were both standing there in their shirts, he turned her around and penetrated her. Not so rough, said Jill, you're hurting me. But Hubert seemed not to hear. In the mirror she caught a glimpse of his eyes, they were glazed like a drunk's.

Be gentle, she whispered, I haven't slept with a man in a long time.

During the early days in the club she had had occasional affairs with guests, and for one season she and the chef had been an item. But he had gotten transferred by the club to southern Turkey, and she hadn't wanted to go with him. Over time, she had felt less and less like getting involved with a man and had contented herself with the occasional flirtation.

Hubert moved faster and faster, then he groaned, jerked once or twice, and collapsed heavily against her. After a while he picked himself up and stepped away from her. Jill could feel the sperm trickling down her leg.

Come on, she said and took him by the hand.

It was dark in the theater, the only light was from the green emergency exit signs. They lay in the bed that stood on the edge of the stage.

Are you sure no one will come in? whispered Hubert.

Don't worry, said Jill, no one before the cleaners in the morning. They embraced and kissed, then Jill sat on top of Hubert and pulled her chemise over her head. It was strange, making love onstage. Jill shut her eyes and moved slowly. Hubert lay very still now. When she opened her eyes once briefly, she saw him looking up at her with a startled expression.

Gillian was seventeen. She was standing by the window of the vacation home with her bare elbows propped on the rough sill, looking up at the sky. The night was full of noises and smells. She was in love, at that time she was often in love, little things were enough to get her dreaming as well as stop the dreams. Everything that happened to her seemed to turn into feeling right away.

She shut the window and went down the stairs. The house was locked, but you didn't need a key to leave it. It was cool outside. She was barefoot and wasn't wearing a jacket, and she was freezing, but that was part of it too. She walked along the road toward the river, ready at any time to duck among the grass if a car passed. After a while the road entered a wood, not much farther to go now. She hardly saw anything in the wood and had to walk more slowly. From the main road on the other side of the gully she heard the occasional car, but there were things closer at hand that she heard too, in the wood, as though the darkness was subtly moving, a little quiver in the atmosphere. When she got to the serpentines that led down to the river, she could already make out the hotel lights. The forest was thinner here, and she could see farther. She ran along the tight curves and over the bridge, the soles of her feet scorched by the rough asphalt.

She walked around the big building, past the brightly lit entrance. As she turned the corner, she heard voices and laughter. The door to the kitchen stood open, where the cooks worked in their white tunics and checked pants. They were just tidying up now. It took a while before one of the trainees, a boy with long hair, saw her. He went to the door, said hello, and offered her a cigarette.

We're almost finished, he said, and lit one himself. Then he stuck his head back in the kitchen and called out: Hey, Edo, your girlfriend's here!

She liked the sound of that. She was Edo's girlfriend, even though she had only met him a week ago, in the pub by the railway station. He had bought her a beer and told her about working in the hotel.

She had arranged with her father that he would come and pick her up at half past ten. When she told Edo, he made fun of her. She always had the feeling he didn't quite take her seriously. He was in his fourth year as a trainee chef, so he was three years older than her, and even had his own car, an old rust bucket of a Fiat. When she went to the pub the following day, she told her father there was no need to collect her, someone would drive her home. He wanted to know who, and they had a fight about it. Edo wasn't in the pub that evening, and she had to walk home, it was over an hour. The next day she plucked up all her courage, went to the hotel after lunch, and asked for Edo. He was standing beside the back door smoking with a couple of his colleagues. She went up to the men, pretending she had turned up by chance. It was his hour off, said Edo, with a complacent smirk. Do you want to see my room? There was great hilarity among the others. He blushed. She said if he liked they could go for a walk.

As soon as she was alone with Edo, he behaved quite differently. Even his voice changed, got quieter and more careful. They walked along the riverbank, the path led through tall grass and bushes, and it was so narrow they had to go Indian file. Gillian went ahead and felt Edo's eyes on her back. After a couple hundred yards, they sat down on the riverbank in the shade of some trees. The current was strong, Edo snapped off twigs and dropped them in the water, where they were pulled in as though by some mysterious power and immediately swept away. He told her about his plans. After his military service, he wanted to go abroad, to Africa or Asia. While Gillian was sweating over Latin and math, Edo would be seeing the world. She lay down and shut her eyes and waited for him to kiss her. But Edo went on talking. Their dreams could hardly be more different, but his enthusiasm was infectious. When they walked back, Gillian's arm brushed against some nettles. Edo looked at the reddened place. He hesitated for a moment, then he raised her arm to his mouth and kissed it. It was as though she had been waiting for that moment. She flung her arms around his neck and kissed him.

Edo, called the apprentice again, it's your girlfriend! Then he turned to her and said, we're all going swimming together, do you feel like coming?

Swimming? Now? She laughed disbelievingly.

Edo stepped out and kissed her on the mouth. They smoked silently. One after the other, the cooks emerged from the kitchen, said goodbye, and disappeared into the darkness. The last to go was the head chef. Don't forget to lock up, he said to Edo, he was making him responsible.

Come on, said Edo to her and to his colleague, once the boss was gone. Inside there were three trainees busy cleaning and wiping, a big fellow with a pimply face, a smaller boy who looked like he was still a kid, and a round girl with thin braids.

Come on, said Edo again. They all went into the storeroom for two liter bottles of cooking wine. Edo went on ahead down narrow passages, then they passed through a metal door and found themselves in a corridor of the hotel. Edo stopped in front of a door labeled SWIMMING BATHS.

It was pitch-black inside and smelled of chlorine. Gillian felt someone take her hand and guide her. Careful, steps. Then they were suddenly standing in front of the pool. A little moonlight came in through the big plate glass windows. Outside she could sense the park, big trees and shrubbery. When she turned, she saw the others were already undressing. The boys let their clothes fall on the floor and ran hunched over to the pool and dropped into it. From the water they looked tensely at the two girls. The cook was still in her underclothes, she had enormous breasts and wide hips. She got completely undressed, and with unexpected grace walked over to the pool and down the steps into the water. The boys had turned to her, and together they swam to the glass wall at the far end. Gillian took advantage of the moment to take her clothes off too and get in the water. Edo left the group and swam over to her. She only had a vague memory of the next hour, kisses and touchings and whisperings. The other trainees climbed out of the water, they chased each other around the pool, careful not to make any noise. She watched the boy with long hair wrestling with the fat girl, who broke away and ran off a few paces, wheezing with laughter. The boy caught up to her, there was more wrestling. Later on they disappeared down a corridor in the darkness. The two other trainees stretched out on deck chairs and passed the wine bottles back and forth. Edo kissed Gillian's throat, and instantly she forgot the others. She shut her eyes, he put his arms around her, she let him, but she didn't dare touch him. He stopped kissing her, laid his head on her shoulder, as though he didn't need it anymore. She couldn't see his face, but she felt his hand. She was lifted up till she was almost on the surface of the water. Suddenly a brief, stabbing pain, and he was inside her. She didn't feel pleasure, but she could feel her body as rarely before. Afterward there was an emptiness in her that hadn't previously existed.

She pushed off from the wall and swam to the steps. Edo came after her. Side by side they sat on one of the top steps in the shallows, paddling at the water with their hands, which touched sometimes as though by chance. I love you—had he said, or had she wanted him to? I love you, she whispered, and he, I love you too. Suddenly there was blue light everywhere, she didn't know what was happening, then she saw that it came from the water. One of the trainees had switched on the underwater lighting. The other leapt up from his deck chair and ran over to him, wine bottle in hand, and the two fought over the light switch. They kept interrupting their struggle to take a pull on the bottle. Edo had turned onto his front. She saw her body and his glow yellowishly, only the parts that were outside the water were gray. The water seemed viscous, oily, spilling over her belly. She hoped it would get dark again, she felt Edo going away from her in the light. She wanted to draw him to her, but he freed himself and stepped out of the pool. He hissed at the two fighters and switched the light off, but he didn't go back in the pool.

A quarter of an hour later, they said goodbye outside the staff rooms. The apprentice with the long hair was snogging the fat girl. The others would surely go on drinking into the early hours.

I have to go home, said Gillian. Edo didn't even ask her if she wanted to come up to his room. He kissed her, but it felt different from before.

Barefoot and with wet hair, she ran home. The next day she had a cold.

Oh, that's nice, said Jill and she went on moving. When she had come and opened her eyes, she could feel a tear running down her cheek. Hubert asked if anything was the matter. Nothing, she said, and laughed, I'm happy.

They were lying side by side when they heard the door to the dressing room.

Someone's just thrown their costumes down on the floor and left them, said a man's voice.

Jill pulled the covers over their heads, and they waited

breathlessly for the voices to go away. Then they stood up, crept back into the dressing room, and quickly put on their clothes.

Their having slept together changed their lives less than Jill had expected, it was as though the nights were a different world into which they dived together. The next morning Jill had only a dreamy recollection of the night just past. When they made love, Hubert always wanted to leave the light on. He didn't take his eyes off her when she got undressed. His hands went all over her body. Sometimes he got up to look at her from a distance, or he would bend her knees and spread her legs like a doctor checking the flexibility of a joint, until, half laughing, half irritably, she would grab him by the hair and pull him to her and kiss him. His kisses were chaste like a child's, as if he were far away and unattainable. He moved and swung her around like an object. Sometimes she had to tell him not to be rough with her. The nicest moments were when they lay there side by side, touching each other abstractedly. Once she asked him if he had found her desirable when he painted her back then.

Of course I did, he said, maybe that's why I didn't succeed in painting you.

And now? she asked.

Why should I paint you? You're here.

A few days later he asked if it would bother her if Lukas came up here on vacation. Jill didn't know what to say, the idea made her a little bit nervous.

Astrid would bring him, he said.

Does she know about me? asked Jill.

Yes, he said, but not that we knew each other before.

Hubert and Jill drove down to the station to collect Lukas.

You didn't say she was bringing her boyfriend, said Jill.

That's because I didn't know, said Hubert angrily, and went off to welcome Astrid, Lukas, and Rolf.

During the ride back there was silence. Only Astrid made an effort at conversation. She talked to Hubert as to an invalid, praised the beauty of the scenery and the weather as though they were all his doing. She made no mention of their last visit. While Astrid spoke, she leaned forward. Rolf and Lukas clowned around behind Astrid's back. Jill parked outside the house.

Come on, said Hubert to Lukas, I'll show you your room.

The two of them disappeared upstairs. Astrid and Rolf followed Jill.

Why don't we sit outside for a bit?

Astrid asked what work Jill did.

I'm in charge of entertainment in the vacation club next to the cultural center.

Astrid asked what that involved, but her interest didn't seem very deep. I've never gone to such a club, what kind of people take their holidays like that?

Rolf said he had gone to a club once when he was a young man. Loads of singles, and a party every night. Fun, I suppose.

People who don't know what to do with themselves, said Astrid.

For a moment, Jill felt sorry for Rolf.

In our club we mostly get families with children, she said. Recently, Hubert's started giving painting classes there.

Oh! said Astrid, apparently genuinely taken aback.

There was silence. Astrid stretched out and sighed, as though to prove that she felt at ease. After a while, Hubert and Lukas came out of the house holding hands.

What train were you going to take? asked Hubert.

I haven't picked one yet, said Astrid.

The trains always leave at twenty of, said Hubert, if we hurry, you can be on the next one.

Shouldn't we take a little walk? asked Astrid. Seeing as we've come all the way up here.

Rolf pulled a map out of his rucksack and said he had seen there was a power place very close by, he wouldn't mind seeing that. Hubert rolled his eyes, but Jill said that was a good idea.

You don't believe in that flummery, do you? asked Hubert.

It's nothing you have to believe in, said Rolf. Most of those places are just very beautiful and have a special resonance.

They walked along the road for a while, then followed a narrow path into a small dip and then up a slope. There, surrounded by a wooden fence, was a large boulder exhibiting many small indentations.

That's a stone with cup and ring marks, said Rolf, you find them all over Europe. Presumably they were prepared by Bronze Age people for purposes of worship. Look, here's a zodiac.

And there was a wheel with spokes etched into the stone, though, admittedly, it didn't look terribly ancient. Jill traced it with her finger. Rolf silently contemplated the stone.

Well, feel anything? asked Hubert with a grin.

Take your time, said Rolf amiably enough. You need to find a silent place in your thoughts. You won't see your reflection in a rapidly flowing stream.

While Rolf was inspecting the rock, Astrid stood silently by. She seemed to be thinking about something. Lukas had run farther on up the slope. There were a few stunted birches up there. He had sat in the grass and was looking down at the grown-ups. Jill wondered what the little boy made of them. When she'd been a girl she had known power places long before she had understood what they were, places she had withdrawn to, that had a significance for her that no one outside could grasp.

It's all about creating a hierarchy of space, said Rolf to Hubert—surely that's what you do as an artist, isn't it?

On their way back, Astrid involved Jill in a conversation, and they walked so slowly that the two men were away off by themselves in no time. Lukas kept running back and forth between the two couples, till Astrid told him to stay with them. Rolf and his father had something to discuss. When they caught up to the men outside the house, Jill looked questioningly at Hubert. Then Rolf and Astrid said goodbye to Lukas, and Hubert drove them to the station.

Jill suggested a game to the boy, or offered to read him a story, but he shook his head and disappeared inside.

When Hubert returned, she asked him what Rolf had had to discuss with him.

Search me, said Hubert. It was something about reconciliation. I told him I couldn't see us getting reconciled as I didn't have a problem with him. Then we talked about Astrid. I wonder how much longer they'll be together.

She sounded me out, said Jill. She wanted to know how long we've been together and how we got to know each other, all those sorts of things. I almost had the sense she was jealous.

Of course she's jealous, said Hubert. What did you tell her?

That you're happy, said Jill.

The two weeks with Lukas went by quickly. Jill was amazed how much time Hubert had for the boy. Often they went hiking, or in the evening they told her how they had spent the whole day damming a mountain stream or clambering around on some rocks. Sometimes they came into the club and visited her in her office or swam in the pool. When Hubert was teaching his course, Lukas played with the visiting children. As the only Swiss kid, he was quite a hit with his funny accent. On days that Jill had off, they went on trips together. Lately, there had been some sightings of the bear that was supposed to be in the area. Lukas often asked about it, he seemed to be at once afraid of it and fascinated by it. Every time he heard something rustle, the boy asked if it was the bear.

Sure, said Hubert, he's coming after us.

Don't frighten him, said Jill.

Lukas only calmed down once they were above the tree line. While Hubert and Lukas went scrambling over the rocks, Jill dropped off to sleep. When she opened her eyes, the sky overhead seemed almost black, although the sun was still shining. There was no sign of Hubert or Lukas, only sometimes she heard a laugh or shout in the distance. It seemed to her as though her accident had never happened. She was married with a child and had a perfectly normal life, like everyone else. The past years were an illusion, the life of somebody else.

That evening she put Lukas to bed for the first time. She told him off for skimping on brushing his teeth and watched as he slipped into his pajamas. Then she had to help him look for his teddy bear, and he wanted to hear all about the real bear again.

Have you seen him ever? he asked.

No, said Jill. He's very shy, he likes to stay out of sight.

Doesn't he have a family, then? asked the boy.

No, said Jill, I think he's still a juvenile. He's just exploring. He's curious about the world. I think bears like to be by themselves.

I don't, said Lukas.

I don't either, said Jill. She kissed the boy on the forehead and called Hubert.

When Lukas was picked up at the end of two weeks by Astrid, Hubert seemed to be less affected than Jill. She had said goodbye to him after breakfast and gone to the office, but she was unable to concentrate on her work. She stood by the window and looked out onto the grounds. We are all one big family here, her boss liked to say. For a week or two at a time they lived that illusion, on "*du*" terms, taking their meals together around big tables, playing sports and guessing games, flirting with each other. But on the day of departure, it all fell apart. At breakfast the guests were in a hurry, the parents were short with their children for not getting a move on, there was a line at reception, because they all wanted to pay their bill, and the lobby was full of islands of luggage on which the children sat like little castaways. Many went off without saying goodbye. At noon, there was a hush over the whole place, meanwhile the maids were working frantically upstairs, removing the traces of the departed. In the afternoon the next load of visitors arrived, and everything started all over again.

Jill went home earlier than usual. Hubert was sitting in the garden, sketching. When she went up to him, he shut the pad with a clack.

There, we've got our peace and quiet back again, he said. Would you like a glass of wine? He told her he'd had lunch with Astrid, and she had told him her relationship with Rolf was at a crisis. I don't know what the problem is, he said, she didn't want to say anything in front of Lukas, and just dropped hints. I think he wants children, and she doesn't. He seems to be the conventional one in that relationship. An esoteric and a square.

Is it square to want children? asked Jill.

She's just too old for him, said Hubert, I told her that all along.

And does Astrid want you back now? asked Jill.

So what if she does? said Hubert after a brief hesitation, as though the possibility had only just occurred to him.

The semester starts in a month, he said over breakfast. Jill looked at him and didn't say anything. The college only needs me to be there a couple of days a week, he said, three at the most. The rest of the time I could spend here. What do you think?

She nodded. If that's what you want.

Hubert would drive down on Wednesday evening and come back just after midnight on Friday, on the last train. When Jill picked him up at the station in the car, he was in a good mood, talking about the students, his time with Lukas, visits to galleries and cinemas. After the vacation, there were fewer guests at the hotel, and the painting course was suspended, but that left Hubert time to get on with his own work. When Jill asked him about it, he was evasive. He didn't like talking about a current project, he said. In the evenings, he withdrew. He had set up a kind of studio in Jill's old room upstairs. He would disappear into there while Jill read or watched TV. Around midnight she would knock on Hubert's door. He stuck his head out, gave her a kiss, and said he'd be along in a minute. She undressed and brushed her teeth. She stood in front of the mirror for a long time waiting, but Hubert didn't come.

In mid-September he said he needed to stay in the city for a while, the term was beginning, and there was lots of organizational stuff to take care of.

How long? asked Jill.

I can't tell you yet, maybe a week or ten days.

Why didn't you tell me sooner? she asked. That way I could have gotten used to the idea a bit.

At night she dreamed of Matthias for the first time in ages. They had a child together, a boy who looked like Lukas. In the morning she couldn't remember any details, she was left with just a picture, a family photograph of her and Matthias in mountain scenery, and the boy between them.

Hubert phoned every other day. He didn't have much to say for himself, and Jill didn't know what to say either.

Things are the same, she said, will you be coming on Saturday?

Yes, he said, almost certainly.

You can come whenever you want, she said, but I'd just like to know first.

She felt worse after that call than before. She had taken Saturday off but still got up early. She spent more time than usual in her bath. She wasn't a particularly gifted or enthusiastic cook, but she wanted to make a welcome feast for Hubert. The village butcher recommended the beef pot roast and explained how to prepare it. Back at home, she put the meat on to cook and laid the table and decorated it with the few remaining flowers she could find in the garden. When everything was ready, the phone rang. It was Hubert. He said he wouldn't be coming today after all. He hadn't been able to call her any earlier. Astrid wasn't doing well, she needed him.

Are you with her now? she asked.

I need to go, he said.

Jill sat in front of the house, but it was cooler than she expected and she went back inside. She started to clean the house. When she took Hubert's dirty clothes down to the laundry room, she sniffed them, and that settled her a bit. She tried to imagine what it would be like on her own again. In a few years she'd be fifty, and for the first time she had the sense that it was too late for certain things in her life.

She vacuumed the stairs. Outside Hubert's workroom she hesitated. Since he had moved in there, she had hardly set foot in the place, she didn't want to bother him, or pressure him. She switched off the vacuum and opened the door. The sudden silence unsettled her, it was like the silence of childhood seeping out of the room and wrapping her up. Jill was about to close the door when she changed her mind and sat down in the threadbare armchair in the corner. The room looked almost the way it had when she was a child. Hubert had left hardly any traces of his occupation, only he had cleared the table, and there were some piles of books, notebooks, and sketch pads on the floor. The ceiling lamp gave a weak yellowish light. She went over to the desk and opened a pad that was lying there. She picked up a pencil, as though she were going to sketch something herself. The pages of the book were covered with pencil cross-hatching. Some were so heavy that they formed shiny reflective surfaces, and you couldn't see the individual lines anymore, still they had a spatial effect. Other pages seemed to be unfinished, they looked like dream landscapes, like maps, a juxtaposition of small crosshatched spaces going in different directions and forming unpredictable patterns with their occasional intersections. Jill hadn't a clue what to make of these drawings. Were they artworks or desperate attempts to kill time? As she leafed on, she saw that it was the block with the nude drawings Hubert had done of her the first time he had stayed the night here. Presumably they weren't anything special, just quick sketches. Not one of them was intact, it looked as though Hubert had crossed them all out before he had embarked on the cross-hatching. Jill was suddenly convinced that he wouldn't be back.

She started covering one of the sketches with her own hatchings, the one of her kneeling on the bed with her hands behind her back, as though chained. The pencil was too hard, so she took another one. She deleted the picture, as though burying her unprotected body under a layer of graphite, making a fossil that no one would ever discover.

It was almost midnight. Jill took off her socks and stepped out of the house barefoot. The air was cool, and the ground under her feet was cold. She walked down the road. A couple of years ago they had built a new bridge over the gorge, but she took the old way. The road down into the gorge was blocked off, in the spring floods there had been a landslide and the underpinnings needed to be secured. Jill scrambled over the barrier and walked past the machines that stood around like sleeping animals. There were lights on in some of the rooms in the cultural center, and the hotel was lit up as well. She crossed the meadow to the annex where the pool was. It had been rebuilt when the club took over the building. She peered in through the big windows, but she couldn't see anything except the glimmer of some light switches. She leaned against the cold glass and looked out at the starry sky. Someone must have opened a window, because there was music coming from the hotel. Today it was Captain Jack Sparrow's turn again, *The Curse of the Black Pearl*. Jill was freezing. She remembered she had a spare jacket in her office. She went around the annex to the main entrance.

Sitting at reception was a young Greek boy who had started there this season and whose name Jill couldn't seem to remember. He asked her if she was going to the open-air concert. She said she had just stepped in to collect something from her office. When she came down in her wool jacket and a pair of sandals she slopped around in at work, a couple of employees were standing in the hallway. They wore colorful clothes and looked as though they were in disguise. The men greeted Jill rambunctiously.

Are you coming to the open-air? asked Ursina.

She was one of the few who came from here, she could even speak Romansh, but she was down on the locals and seemed to prefer the hotel to the village.

I don't know, said Jill, I just came in to pick something up.

Oh, come on, said the masseuse and put her arm around Jill. When did you last dance?

At reception a couple of the men were teasing the Greek boy, who was on night duty and who therefore couldn't come with them. Outside a minibus drew up.

Marcos is driving, said Ursina. Jill was pulled along by the others and finally clambered into the bus.

173

They took the main road up the valley. Marcos had put on a CD, a tinny-sounding guitar with a melancholy woman's voice. From the backseats the men complained—wasn't there any other music?—but the driver ignored them. Jill, on the front seat, asked what the music was.

Fado, he said, from Portugal, Amália Rodrigues.

And what is she singing?

Marcos didn't say anything, at first Jill thought he didn't understand her question, but then she realized he was listening. When the guitar was playing on its own, he embarked on his halting translation.

What a strange way my heart has to live. Lonesome heart, independent heart, not for me to command. If you don't know where you're going, why do you want to run.

That's nice, said Ursina.

Her voice was very near. Jill saw that she had craned forward to listen. Marcos didn't say anything. Only when they turned off the main road after half an hour and followed a narrow little mountain road into a side valley, did he ask what sort of concert they were going to.

It's a Goa party, said Gregor, a young cook, from the backseat. Trance, you know.

He explained the difference between the various techno forms to Marcos. Jill didn't listen, she was so tired her eyes were falling shut. They passed a village, and a little later a spectrally illuminated campsite. There were torches stuck in the ground, big fires were burning, and some of the brightly colored tents were lit from inside. Marcos slowed to walking pace. In the headlights Jill saw strange figures walking up or coming down the mountain, some were moving as though dancing, others had drooping shoulders. Finally they got to the entrance of the festival area. You couldn't see the stage from there, but you could already hear the music, a monotonous *boom-boom-boom*. Marcos asked what time he should come back for them.

Tomorrow morning, Ursina said, laughing.

Someone said they would make it back on their own. There were shuttle buses. Suddenly everyone dispersed, only Ursina was left with Jill, and she took her hand and led her to the entrance.

Even as they approached the stage, Ursina started to move to the music. She had on a crop top, and her hair was in two braids.

Aren't you cold? asked Jill.

She envied Ursina's slim form and suppleness.

Not much farther now, said Ursina, and pulled her through the crowds. Most of the audience was half Jill's age, and she felt badly out of place, but no one seemed bothered by her presence. The feeling was very relaxed. The music was now like a carpet of sound, she could hear sitars, a sort of crunching, and then the voice of an old man saying something in English about visions and peace. The DJ onstage lifted an arm and then made short hacking movements with his hand in the direction of the people, and suddenly a rhythm boomed out. The tones were so low that Jill felt them right through her body and had to put something against them. The people started bopping around on command, a mass of bodies, moving in time. Some rowed with their arms, as though swimming through molasses, others stood almost still, only twitching a shoulder or twisting their heads from side to side. Jill could not escape the rhythm and began dancing in spite of herself. Ursina turned briefly to her, smiled, and with a complicated and yet completely harmonious movement screwed her arms up into the air. Over the stage hung cloth sails lit by black light, the psychedelic patterns that were projected on a screen behind the DJ changed to the pulse of the music. Jill tried to empty her mind. Once, she felt a hand on her shoulder, it was Gregor the cook standing beside her. He was yelling something into her ear, but she couldn't understand a word. At the same time she felt him press something into her hand. Jill looked down and saw a small pill in the flash of a beam. Gregor pointed to his mouth, yelled something else, this time Jill could make out: Fun! and No problem! She hesitated, then put the pill in her mouth. The cook pushed on and laid his hand on the shoulder of Ursina, who was a few feet away. She saw them put their heads together. Then Ursina shook her head, turned to her, and shook it again with a cross expression. Jill shut her eyes and went on dancing. The music seemed to be coming to some sort of climax that never happened. Sometimes the bass stopped, and there were spherical sounds left hanging before a rhythm set up again, sometimes it just accelerated steadily. For a while Jill kept up, then she gave up and drifted, and was pulled into the maelstrom of noises. She had the sense of going floor by floor through a tall building, and everywhere was music, colored lights, and dancing people. Suddenly someone held her. Jill opened her eyes and saw Ursina standing beside her.

Come, said Ursina, you need to rest.

I'm not tired, said Jill.

Ursina took her hand and led her to a stall where they were giving out water.

You need to drink a lot, she said, otherwise you'll keel over.

I need to pee, said Jill.

A long line had formed in front of the toilet huts on the edge of the area. The music was less loud here, and mixed with the sound of a mountain stream flowing past them. Jill must have lost her sandals somewhere, at any rate she was barefoot and she felt the cold dew that had settled on the meadow. She wasn't wearing a watch and had no idea what time it was.

Are you doing all right? asked Ursina.

I haven't felt this good in ages, said Jill.

Where's Hubert? asked Ursina. I haven't seen him lately.

Hubert is history, said Jill.

I like him, said Ursina, he's an amazing painter. Suddenly Jill's mood swung and she could hardly breathe. Now everything was clear, Hubert had been sleeping with Ursina all along. That was why he had practically stopped painting and had destroyed the nude drawings he had done of her. Presumably Hubert wasn't in the city at all, he was with the masseuse in her apartment. Or he was here at the party somewhere. Ursina looked at her in horror.

What are you talking about? she said. You're insane.

Jill closed her eyes, she felt dizzy. She was almost falling over, but Ursina took her in her arms and helped her to sit.

I'm sorry, said Jill, and she hugged Ursina.

What are you sorry about?

I don't know, said Jill, everything. I'm sorry about everything. I need to pee again. She had to laugh.

You haven't been yet, said Ursina.

Jill went on dancing. Sometimes she stood still, only moving her head and her shoulders. Or she flew over the landscape without beating her wings. Clouds blew past her in accelerated motion. She dipped into a blue sea, saw underwater landscapes, schools of fish shooting concertedly at incredible speed in and out of bright coral. She seemed to be always a fraction of a second ahead of the music, her movements were producing the music, controlling it. The beats shaped the room, they felt like huge invisible bubbles flying toward her and bouncing off her. The dancers had lifted their arms and kept pushing the bubbles away into the air, they flew higher and higher, floating over the dark valley. Far below she could see the wood, the railway line, and the road. The music grew quieter and finally gave way to the monotonous pouring of the wind. Jill saw snowcapped peaks, then chains of mountains, one behind the other, and in between them green valleys, the Po basin with its sleeping towns, and in the distance the lights of the port cities and the black plain of the sea. She no longer felt the weight and shelter of the mountains, she had the feeling of weightlessness to which she surrendered without fear.

When she opened her eyes, she was lying on the ground with her head in Ursina's lap. Someone had covered her with a windbreaker. In front of them was a big flickering fire and some people Jill didn't know. Her thoughts were clearer.

Won't the music ever stop? she asked. What time is it?

Ursina shook her head and looked at her watch. Half past three.

Where are the others?

I've no idea, said Ursina. They'll find their way back, don't worry about them.

Jill sat up. I don't want to go back, she said, not knowing what she meant. I want to know what was in the pill that Gregor gave me.

Some shit or other, said Ursina, you should be more careful. Have you really finished with Hubert?

He has with me, said Jill. Oh, I've no idea, maybe he hasn't. He's with his ex-wife, apparently she's not doing well. I don't think he'll come back.

I can't imagine that, said Ursina.

Jill laughed. And why not?

Because you're the most lovable person I've ever met, said Ursina. If I was into women, you'd be my first choice. She looked Jill in the eyes. I mean it, you're the spirit of the club, everyone says so. I know a couple of people in the village who think you're a bit strange, but that's only because you have such a quiet life.

Ursina got up and said, come on, let's dance, I'm getting cold.

The crowd in front of the stage was hardly any smaller than before. Another DJ was now spinning, but the music was identical. Ursina stayed close to Jill. They bought something to eat at a stall, a vegetarian dish with Oriental spices, mushy and overcooked, and then they danced some more. The sky slowly brightened. Ursina tapped Jill on the shoulder and pointed up at the peaks that were

glowing red in the first beams of the sun. The other dancers had noticed it too, some just stood still and looked. Jill
and Ursina had made their way to the edge of the crowd
and watched the light slowly wander down the mountain
slopes until at last it reached the festival area.

I think I'll go home, said Jill. I don't have as much stam-
ina as you.

Do you want me to go with you? asked Ursina.

Jill shook her head. I can make my own way.

She took a shuttle bus down to the train station. There
were a couple of tired characters on the bus, one or two
of them looked unwell. No one spoke, silence was a tonic
at the end of the noisy night. Jill felt very sober and clear-
headed, as though she had woken up from a long period
of unconsciousness. At the station she got coffee from a
machine and sat down on the platform in the sun. She
looked at her filthy feet. The bottom of her skirt was dirty
as well. In the train she thought about what Ursina had
said. She felt like a child found in a game of hide-and-seek.
After the breathless excitement of being hidden, it felt like
a relief, she could move freely again, everything had just
been a game. For six years she had hidden herself up here
and not even noticed that no one was looking for her. Over
time she had felt so comfortable in her hiding place that
it felt like the whole of life. Only in spring, when the snow
refused to melt, did she sometimes think of moving back
to the city. Perhaps the reason she had asked Hubert to put
on a show at the cultural center was so that he could get
her out of this life that wasn't hers. That's what she would

say to him if he came back: You should do whatever you want, you don't owe me anything.

She transferred onto the bus. The driver said good morning and something about the weather. In the front row sat an old woman with a traveling bag, who was the only other passenger. She and the driver talked in Romansh. Jill didn't understand. She was thinking that before long the larches would change color, that the first snow would come soon, and then stay until March or April. She couldn't imagine getting through another winter here alone, the cold days and long nights.

The bus stop was about two hundred yards from her house. As Jill walked along the road, she mapped out the day ahead. She would shower and wash her hair, then sit in the garden with cappuccino and a cigarette and read the Sunday paper. She probably wouldn't eat anything at lunchtime, the vegetarian dish was still heavy in her stomach, and she had a funny taste in her mouth. Perhaps she would go into the office briefly in the afternoon and take care of something, just so as not to feel so useless, and maybe have a little chat with someone. The new guests would be standing around uncertainly, because they didn't yet know their way around the building and weren't used to the rules of the club. We all call each other by first names. The pool? That's along the corridor and down the stairs. Dinner is anytime after half past six. The winner of the Trivial Pursuit quiz will be announced afterward. I hope you have a very enjoyable stay here. She tried to work out what time Hubert might arrive, if he set off early, if he breakfasted first with Astrid and Lukas, if he waited until after lunch.

Jill stood under the shower, washed the dirt off her feet, and suddenly she knew she would give up her job and leave here. Not immediately, there was no hurry. Perhaps Hubert would come with her and they would make a new start together somewhere, but her decision had nothing to do with his. The game was over, she was free and could go anywhere.

Keep in touch with
Granta Books:

Visit grantabooks.com to discover more.

GRANTA

Also available from Granta Books
www.grantabooks.com

SEVEN YEARS

Peter Stamm

Translated by Michael Hofmann

'*Seven Years* is a novel to make you doubt your own
dogma. What more can a novel do than that?'
Zadie Smith

Alex is caught between two very different women. Sonia,
his wife, is intelligent, beautiful, charming, and ambitious.
Together they have established a prestigious architecture
firm and a life of luxury. But long hours and failed attempts
at starting a family bring about the seven-year itch, and
soon Alex begins an affair with dull, passive Ivona, with
devastating consequences.

'A quietly shattering meditation on the depths of desire'
The Times

'I love this novel ... It has the makings of an existential classic'
Sunday Telegraph

'Cool and immensely accomplished'
Adam Mars-Jones, *Observer*

'Quietly spectacular'
New Yorker

Also available from Granta Books
www.grantabooks.com

WE'RE FLYING

Peter Stamm

Translated by Michael Hofmann

SHORTLISTED FOR THE FRANK O'CONNOR
INTERNATIONAL SHORT STORY AWARD

'An extraordinary author who can make the ordinary
absolutely electrifying ... Hard to recommend too highly'
'Books of the Year', *The Times*

In this astute, beautifully composed collection, a woman
becomes involved with her younger upstairs neighbour; a man
waits for the outcome of medical tests; and a young couple
learns to navigate the thrills and complications of cohabitation.
A master of the short story, Stamm does not spare the reader's
feelings, nor does he waste a word.

'There is something extraordinary in Stamm's ability to make
normal situations, described in such minimalist prose, so
engrossing and affecting ... Hofmann's translation is precise
and irresistibly readable'
Prospect

'Original, assured and utterly beguiling'
Daily Mail

'One of Europe's most exciting writers ... a writer
to read, and read often'
New York Times